Bo

Caught
Caught
Caught on Camera: Part Three
Caught on Camera: Part Four
Caught on Camera: Part Five

Christmas Crackers

Candy Canes and Coal Dust

Bollywood

The Unwholesome Adventures of Harita

Lust Bites

Escape to the Country

What's Her Secret?

Breathe You In

What's His Passion?

Dark Warrior

Anthologies

Treble
Stand to Attention
Wild Angels

Over the Knee
His Rules

Single Titles

Thief
Orchestrating Manoeuvres
That Filthy Book
Tarzan of the Apes
Who Dares Wins
Burning Rubber
Toy Boy
Rule Breaker
Spicing it Up
Heat of the Day

Books by Natalie Dae

Fantasies Explored

Think Kink
Thinking Kinkier
Kinky Thinking

Marshall Cottage

Master Zum
Master Red
Master Connor
Master Stephen
Master Dan
Master M

Stiff Upper Lip

Minute Maid

Lust Bites

Soul Keeper

Sexy Snax

VampDom
Firecracker

What's Her Secret?

The Submissive's Secret
Denial

Anthologies

Bound to the Billionaire

Single Titles

A Gentleman's Harlot
That Filthy Book
Shades of Grey
Forced Assassin
Rude Awakening
Waiting for Him
Magenta Starling
Shadow and Darkness
Lincoln's Woman

That Filthy Book

ISBN # 978-1-78651-924-5

Interior text design by Claire Siemaszkiewicz

Totally Bound Publishing

Published in 2016 by Totally Bound Publishing, Newland House, The Point, Weaver Road, Lincoln, LN6 3QN, United Kingdom.

Totally Bound Publishing is a subsidiary of Totally Entwined Group Limited.

THAT FILTHY BOOK

LILY HARLEM and
NATALIE DAE

Dedication

Working with Lily is an indulgence. She's super-talented – super all round. I love you, Lovely Lily! – Natalie Dae

Chapter One

I stared at him, this husband of mine, his naked form rendered a silhouette from the brightness of the sun streaming through the hotel room window. The light filtered through his black tousled hair, glinted off his shoulders, giving him a glowing aura. This was our first time alone together since what felt like forever, what with meeting and having children in the blink of an eye. Ten years had passed—where had the time gone?—and here we were, away for two nights just so we could get back to being who we used to be; why we'd become a couple in the first place.

The sun had hung heavy in a blue swathe of cloudless sky earlier, the fiery orb almost lazy in its placement, as though someone had painted a picture and tossed in the yellow ball, not caring where it landed. Funny how the sky could be deceptive, making a person think it was hot outside when it was cold enough to freeze the balls off a brass monkey. Faint, puffy clouds had appeared since I'd first woken, too, and I marvelled at the way my body had gone back to its old, pre-children habits. Waking, having sex, dozing off again.

Now—around noon—it was time to get up, go out and do something, I supposed, but what I didn't know. I didn't have any energy for anything much beyond another languid fuck. A tress of my long blonde hair tickled my bare breast, the ends teasing my nipple. It sparked desire inside me again, and I wondered if my body would ever get enough this weekend. God, I'd been insatiable since we'd arrived last night. Perhaps shirking off the shackles of motherhood, of the responsibilities that came with the job, had freed my mind and allowed me to abandon everything. I had become what I once was—a woman who enjoyed a hot night of sex with her man, not giving a hoot whether her screams of pleasure could be heard; whether the banging of the headboard would wake someone.

But I hadn't shaken them off. Not really. They still lingered, a shadow of feelings, whispers of our children's laughter, thinking I could hear them calling me… Tess and Lucy, our two wonderful little girls. And then there were whispers of my fantasies, ones I'd held in check since I'd read a sexy book many years ago. Ones that had made me think I was dirty for wanting them. When I'd first met Jacob, I'd shoved away the feelings of guilt and let the fantasies surface, briefly. Our rampant sex had been too enjoyable, too damn hot to allow myself to dwell on whether what we did was right, but as the years had rolled by and I'd become embroiled in motherhood, kinky sex had fallen by the wayside, and the old trappings had moved in permanently. We can't do this because we're parents. We can't do that because of the girls. We can do that because it's too *rude*…

I stared at my surroundings to force my thoughts in another direction. The room wasn't much, just a double bed with white sheets and a beige quilt. Low cabinets either side, the perfunctory wardrobe and a sideboard, all in light wood that matched the colour of the quilt and walls. A sea of beige. But it suited our needs. The decoration hadn't exactly been on our minds when we'd stumbled through the door last night. Ripping one another's clothes off had been the order of the evening.

"What are you thinking?" Jacob asked, remaining at the window.

And there he was, not even a flicker of movement indicating that he'd turned around. Just him, standing there, a god in front of a glass pane. I studied his reflection instead of responding, squinting to make out the faint, fine taper of hairs that ran from his belly button down to the curly thatch nestled above his cock. A long cock that was semi-hard, heavy-looking, and eminently touchable. I loved the feel of it in my hand, the way my fingers curled around its width, the softness of his skin on mine. A thrill ran through me at the thought of it, and I folded my arms across my breasts in an effort to stop me from fondling them. But why shouldn't I? Too many nights we'd hurried, coming together in a rush before the inevitable interruptions came. Too many nights I'd denied myself the pleasure of having Jacob inside me.

'Mum, I want a drink of water. Mum, I can't sleep…'

Stop thinking of them. You promised yourself you wouldn't do that.

And I had, but casting aside the parental mantle wasn't as easy as I'd told Jacob it would be. Wasn't as easy as flicking a switch. They crept in, the two girls we'd created – smiling faces filling my mind, eclipsed by their worried expressions that made me think they weren't coping well without us.

They're with Jacob's mum and dad. They'll be fine.

My determination that we could do this had persuaded Jacob to come away with me. It had been a big thing, this, leaving the children behind, but if we hadn't done it now we never would.

"Is it the kids?" he asked.

"No."

I didn't lie often, but if I admitted my thoughts then he would tag onto the worry bandwagon and we'd end up going home. I didn't want that. I wanted the rest of the day, the night, and the majority of tomorrow morning to be just me and him. It wasn't too much to ask, was it? Not after ten years of being devoted and never going out to the pub, never leaving them…

"I was thinking about us," I said, throwing the sheet away from my body and sitting up. I stretched; a fingers-pointing-to-the-ceiling kind of stretch that chased away all the kinks and left me loose-limbed and pliant.

Pliant.

Now there was a word that brought a rush of desire to

my cunt. Pliant made me think of suppleness, of legs and arms twisted in difficult positions, of torsos arched and backs curved. Jacob was pliant, always had been, and once upon a time I'd been able to bend with the best of them. But now, after the kids and getting out of my workout routine, a little weight had settled on my bones, preventing me doing all those delicious things I used to do. Like bending over to touch my toes and being taken from behind. Like widening my legs to such a degree it was as though I was being *forced* into that position. Not that I had been forced, but it was something I thought about every so often. Him taking me against my will, a scenario that thrilled me more than it perhaps should have. Just a little fantasy to keep me warm when Jacob worked away. And the book I'd read had planted it into my mind, yet I'd tried to forget what rested between the front and back covers, telling myself it just wasn't proper to want such things.

"What about us?" he asked, lacing his hands behind his head and jutting his abdomen out until his cock almost touched the glass.

"Someone could see you like that, you know." I'd avoided his question because...hell, I'd grown shy somehow, grown out of being able to tell him exactly what was on my mind. It made me feel embarrassed to say I'd been recalling the days when we'd fucked for hours, sweat-soaked and sore, falling asleep only to wake for more of the same. My mind had also wandered to the forced entry thing, hadn't it? A flicker of fast images shooting across the air in front of me as though they were the real thing. Rough and ready sex. Pleasure-pain. Jacob speaking sharply, his hands also abrasive, palms scouring my skin instead of skimming. His cock a relentless shunt instead of a glide. Tongue an insistent probe instead of a gentle exploration.

How come being here had enabled my old self to at first poke me with a tentative finger, but now jabbed with urgent pressure?

"I don't give a shit," he said on a laugh.

It took me a moment to realise what he meant. I thought back to what we'd been talking about. His cock on the glass. Someone seeing. A surge of desire swarmed over me at that. Being watched – was it something I could handle one day? Oh, not having a third person in our life. No, I'm too jealous to share our time together, even if it involved another man. But being somewhere, *knowing* we could possibly have an observer?

I think I could. Maybe.

"We're too high up, anyway," he went on.

I smiled at the fact he was oblivious to my thoughts, that he had no idea I had suddenly become someone who wanted a whole lot more from her sex life than what we'd been doing. It wasn't that Jacob was crap in bed, nothing like that, just that... God, I wanted more time to explore, more time full stop. And what the hell would he think about my fantasies anyway? Were they too 'out there' for him? They wouldn't have been years ago, but now...

I wasn't sure I even had the courage to share them.

"Come and stand with me," he said.

"What, *naked?*"

I stood, hesitant to do as he asked. What if someone spotted us and called the police, telling them a couple in The Grand were indecently exposed in the window?

Admit it. Although scary, it is exciting.

"Yes, naked. Come on. All that's out there is the street, and that's way down below. Nothing opposite, unless you count the buildings half the size of this one. We're in a five-hundred-room hotel, love. A tall one."

Sod it. This weekend I was supposed to be my real self, find the woman who'd been lost amidst school runs and after-school clubs. And if I dug beneath the guilt I could feel that the thrill of being naughty, a rebel, was still with me. But what about the girls and...

Stop it.

I walked to the window, stood behind him and peeked around his arm. He was right. Too far up for anyone to see us, yet still it felt too naughty. It was one thing to fantasise about it, but to actually do it... What if someone had binoculars?

"I'm telling you," he said, as though he'd read my mind, "no one will see us. D'you really think anyone would give a toss if they did? They'd probably see us as two dirty, middle-aged people anyway. If they're young, that is. Remember how we used to think that about people our age?"

I cupped my hands around his biceps and pressed my cheek to his back, his skin warm and soothing. He smelt of his recent shower, all flowery hotel soap and alien-smelling shampoo, and the faint aroma of clinically washed towels, totally absent of the scent of my usual fabric softener. Home was intruding again, so I switched the images off.

And yes, I remembered thinking that. Remembered thinking it was gross that older people 'did it'. Yet here we were, older and still doing it. Funny how your perspective changes.

"Hmmm," I said. "But with age comes a better understanding. Love helps, too. It goes deeper than it did years ago, pardon the pun."

He laughed, a low rumble that reverberated through my cheek and sent ripples of lust to my pussy. I wanted him again, hard and fast, no foreplay or sentimental sweet nothings. Just pure, honest fucking. I stared at the way his ear curved, recalled how the lobe felt in my mouth, sweetly soft and fleshy. A wave of love consumed me. How was it possible I could care for him more than I did back then? I thought I loved him as much as I could, full to bursting with adoration and respect, yet every day, every month, each new year brought a stronger connection.

God, I was so damn lucky.

My eyes stung, the emotion getting a better hold on me than I wanted it to. No time for sentimental tears, just time for us. The thought that it would take until tomorrow to fully relax struck me as typical—it would be time to go home and leave this weekend behind. Except this time together would remain in our memories, and we could whisper about it in bed at night when we felt the need to recapture it. I'd have to be content with that because there was no way we could stay here longer. Jacob had work to return to, and the girls had school. His parents were going away on Tuesday, a leisurely cruise in the Mediterranean for a week, and with my parents living in the arse end of nowhere in Scotland, getting them to come down to babysit wasn't an option.

I was a bundle of contradictions, wasn't I? One minute I'd forgotten our home life, the next I hadn't. It was the idle times, that was it—moments where I allowed my mind to wander and think things I shouldn't. Swallowing deeply, I told myself to enjoy what remained of our weekend together—otherwise, I'd regret it later.

"Do you think we ought to do some sightseeing or something?" I asked, wondering, if he'd answer in the affirmative, whether I could muster the energy to get dressed let alone waltz through the nearby park or visit the art museum. We'd promised ourselves an afternoon of appreciating art, gazing at the beauty created by others and discussing how each piece made us feel inside. "We could do," he said. "After."

"After what?" I smiled, my bunching cheek squashed against his shoulder blade, my breasts heated from his skin. The rest of me felt chilled, as though I needed the whole of him wrapped around me, arms and legs a warm embrace.

"After I fuck you against this window."

I gasped, widening my eyes at what he'd said. It seemed he'd returned to his old self more easily than I had. I wanted to answer that he could fuck me against anything he liked, anytime he wanted—he didn't have to ask. He could just grab me, pin me down and forge into me. I wanted it hard and fast, hot and panting, my body at his mercy. Whatever he wanted to do to me, he could.

There it was again, that urge to give up control to him completely. A fuck where I had no say in it. His rules, his pleasure. It flooded my mind like a cloud of dangerous desire.

But again I didn't say anything about handing over control. The words wouldn't come, stuck in my throat as they were, a big ball of unspoken needs that swelled to be released. Pushing, expanding.

"Talk to me," he said. "Like you used to. Dirty and rough. While there's no one but me to hear you."

A sudden bout of insecurity gripped me, a closing fist around my heart, creating a flutter of panic and the inability to breathe properly. I'd been so free and easy before we'd had the girls, so ready to try anything, do anything; caught up in the first flush of love. And now…

"I can't." I squeezed my eyes closed and waited for the feeling to pass.

"Can't?"

He covered my hands with his, the warmth of his touch giving me a jolt of longing. I imagined those hands roving my skin, seeking out my special places, erogenous zones that he knew by heart. My pulse thrummed, loud in my ears, the throb of my heartbeat an almost violent smack against my ribs. I cracked open my eyes, peeked around him to see his fingertips pressed down on my hand, the ends white where he held me so tightly. Did he hold me like that because he'd anticipated a negative answer? A rush of guilt took over me, heating my cheeks and bringing on the need to cry. I was spoiling this, wasn't I—by not keeping to my promise to play the game as though we were free spirits who could do anything we wanted?

"I feel stupid," I said quietly, wanting him to take over, to talk to *me* dirty and remind me how it was done.

Because I had forgotten.

"Stupid? Why?"

His chest inflated, his back rising beneath my face, and he held his breath.

"Because…because I've forgotten how to do it. And if I say what I want, it might not come out right and I'll feel silly."

He turned, just that movement alone soaking my cunt, and cradled me against him. Hands on my back, he rubbed them up and down, the motion soothing, chasing away the goosebumps, giving me the sense that everything would always be all right when he held me like this. He was magic, my husband, this man who had promised to take care of me until the day he died, ensuring I was never sad, never had reason to cry. I was the kind of woman who floundered without him near, who, when panicked or insecure, only needed him to walk in the room and everything bad would melt away.

"You never have to feel silly with me," he said, the words low and reassuring. "Never. I've told you that before. Did you forget that too?"

How could I? He'd said it often enough, and I wondered then whether he got tired of his constant encouragement, of always having to work to make me believe him. He was devoted, I knew that. Knew it deep inside me, where I kept the special memories, the nuggets of love he'd shown me, those private moments between us that no one else knew about. Small touches, glances in a crowded room, even in the supermarket, where the gap between us was too wide and I wanted nothing more than to rush to him, to have his arms about me.

To have the cushioned feeling of being adored.

I embraced him, splaying my palms on his back and resting my cheek on his chest. His heart beat wildly, a manic rhythm that matched mine, as though we both anticipated what was to come. We knew I would give it a try, that I'd utter words I hadn't spoken in years, in a voice that was husky and all kinds of sexy.

We just had to wait for *me* to fully come back. She was there, simmering below the surface, filling my mind with all manner of filthy things—she just needed that extra push to come out, that was all.

"Tell me. Remind me what I used to say," I whispered.

I held my breath, knowing I would blush when he recited words from the past. How had I become so…boring? So shy?

"Ah, that's easy. I'll never forget." He held me tighter, his warmth oozing into my skin like the heat of bath water. "Some days I sit and remember, think about the old days and wish—"

"That I was like that again?"

Oh, God. I've made him as boring as me, having to turn to daydreams in order to get his jollies. How long has he been thinking of the past?

He took a moment before he answered. Weighing up how to phrase it, I'd bet.

"Not necessarily that, no. Just wishing that you'd let yourself go every so often. Not be so good all the time."

"Good?" I lifted my head and stared up at him, into dark brown eyes that melted my knees with their long, thick black lashes. "Is that what I am now? Good?"

God, I *was* boring. I'd slipped into that rut people talked about. The one where the wife became staid and unyielding in the bedroom. Where a bed was just for sleeping, maybe a quick fuck once a month. The rut I'd always vowed never to get into. But that rut was deep; it went so far down that I couldn't see over the damn top when it came to talking dirty. I bristled, knowing exactly what he meant, knowing I ought to keep my mouth shut because I'd let things spill out that weren't intended for him. No, what I wanted to say was a torrent of sentences berating myself, and I couldn't do that, not in front of Jacob. He said it hurt him when I put myself down. Like a physical pain deep inside. If I ranted now, I'd do so knowing I'd upset him.

He stroked my face with both hands, staring down at me as though I was the most precious thing to walk the planet, and I felt wretched. For letting him down. Becoming 'one of those women'. For allowing *us* to change.

"Tell me," I said, disliking the begging tone that rimmed the words. "Come on. Tell me what I used to say. Help me say it again."

I was desperate now, truly desperate to recapture what we'd once had. The thought of how we'd been lately… God, it was shameful. I wanted to say the words so badly, but something blocked their exit. They were all there in my head; delicious, filthy sentences that would make any grandmother's toes curl; ones I'd read in a book many years ago, yet when I opened my mouth to force them out, they lodged in my throat. Frustration added to desperation made me whimper. I felt so helpless, useless, a stupid, insecure bundle of nerves.

He smiled, a stretch of those beautiful lips that showed his straight teeth, all except the one canine that stuck out a little. "Let me see. What did you used to say…?"

My heart contracted with love for him. He was doing what he always did—making everything okay again. Taking the pressure off me and having the burden on *his* shoulders. How the hell had I been so lucky to find him, to keep him? My eyes stung, and I blinked, swallowed hard and prayed the tears wouldn't fall.

He glanced up at the ceiling, a teasing gesture that had me wanting to grasp him around the neck and force his gaze back to me. I wanted to reach up and touch the knobbly scar beside his eye, to brush my thumb down his cheek. His pretence of being deep in thought drove a spike of new frustration into my gut, yet I smiled, because as well as doing this for me, he was playing with me. Enjoying it, too.

"Fuck my cunt," he said, lowering his head so his gaze met mine again. "Fuck my cunt, that's what you used to say. Jacob, come over here and lick my wet pussy." He brushed his lips over mine. "Remember that?"

I blushed—damn it, I knew I would—and memories came flooding back. Me on the bed with my legs open wide, my clit aching, throbbing, the need for him to lick it, suck it into his mouth, so strong it took my breath away. Me bending over the bed, hands on the mattress, feet apart on the rug, begging him to *fuck my cunt* from behind. I'd said those words and more, my God I had, but could I say them again?

He continued. "Jacob, suck my nipples. God, yes, suck them harder. Suck them until they hurt. That's it, baby, bite them. Hold them between your teeth and pull. Harder. Fuck, Jacob, fuck I'm so wet..."

And I was wet now. As I shifted slightly from foot to foot, my labia glided and juices seeped, dampening my inner thighs. My channel clenched, a sharp spasm that coincided with my clit expanding. I dug my nails into his back, drawing them down to his buttocks, and counted to ten. He kissed the top of my head, his hands exploring, casting warming circles on my arse. We stood this way for what seemed a long time, me rolling those words around in my head to test them; see how they sounded years after I'd last spoken them.

"Fuck my cunt," I whispered, tasting the delicious filth of those words on my tongue. "Suck my nipples," said with a little more courage and a little less embarrassment.

"Just a bit louder, love. I didn't quite catch what you said."

I knew he had, knew he was doing what he always did. Encouraging me. Letting me know I could do anything I wanted if I put my mind to it. I lifted my head, a surge of desire swelling my folds, and swallowed the last of my nervousness.

"Do it, Jacob," I said, staring straight at him, a challenge to myself to see this through. "Fuck my cunt and suck my nipples. Hard."

Chapter Two

In what seemed less than half a second, Jacob had spun me around and pressed my back to the window. His big hands were firm and determined and radiated brute strength, the action just rough enough to send yet another wave of giddy excitement through me—that damn book again.

The thick, tempered glass was cold, a shock of ice that brought more goosebumps. My heart was beating so hard and so fast that the sound of my pulse drowned everything out except the rasping of our breath. It was the accompaniment to the dull thuds, a sexy scratch of noise that scuffed the air, our own form of music.

"Fuck, it's good to hear you're back," he said, bending his head to lick up and down the column of my neck. "I've missed you."

God, I'd really let things go, hadn't I? There was no time to ponder that now, because his wet tongue was working wonders on my libido, preventing anything other than what he was doing from filling my mind. His breath heated my skin, raising the hairs on the back of my neck, and a small shiver went through me. It spread inside and out, encompassing me as though it were a live being coming out of hibernation. It left me giddy and hyper-alert, sensitive to everything related to heat—the mugginess of our close proximity, the slowly warming glass at my back and arse, the hotness where our bellies and chests touched.

I clutched his arse, massaging with slow kneads, pulling him towards me a little more so his erection pressed against my lower belly. He was so much taller than me, and the need to have that hard length between my folds prompted me to place my arms around his neck and stand on tiptoe.

"I need to feel your cock on my cunt," I said into his ear, more forcefully than I'd intended. I was still trying on my old self, seeing if it fit me these days, and for a pleased moment I realised it did.

Very well.

Bolder, I went on. "Need it rubbing up and down my slit. Wet from my juices. You like that, right? Yeah, you like it, don't you, Jacob?" I smiled a small smile as he stiffened further, and it gave me courage. "Fuck, yes, you like your cock covered in my wetness. Like me licking it clean." I raised one leg, bent at the knee, indicating I wanted him to pull me, hold me over his rigid length. "Come on, Jacob. Lift me up so I can press my sopping pussy against you."

His sharp intake of air made my smile grow wider, and a stutter of breath huffed out of his mouth and onto my neck. I had him right there, right where I wanted him, and it hadn't taken much effort at all.

Back into the swing of things, growing more daring by the second, and adoring the fact that he was loving my words so much, I said, "I want to get off just by sliding up and down. Just from your fat, wide cock head brushing my clit." The thought of it snatched the air from my lungs for a moment, but I recovered quickly enough to say, "And you remember when we did that before, don't you? Yes, you remember. You came too, my pressure dragging down your foreskin…"

"Jesus, Karen. You're fucking killing me here."

He lifted me, settled my slit against his cock, and grabbed my arse. Pressing down, he applied light force and, my God, I could've come just from that. I buried my head in the crook of his neck, willing myself to calm down. It was difficult, though—my clit throbbed in time with my heart, and that thought returned, the one about someone using binoculars, and I found myself more turned on than ever. This wasn't indecent exposure, it was *decent*—fabulous, exciting and off-the-charts hot.

Not being so 'good' now, was I?

He began to move, sliding and rubbing through my slick folds. I hooked one ankle over the other and gripped as best I could, thankful that he was holding me so tight. I was weak with desire—all my energy had been diverted to my cunt. All I could think of was the pressure of his shaft working over my clit and the sensation of my pussy moistening further for him. It was so wet I imagined it dripping down my thighs, trickling to my knees and soaking onto the plush carpet.

"Talk to me some more," he demanded, his lips just touching my left temple. "God, talk to me some more, love. Talk dirty, talk filthy, whatever comes into your head, just say it. I want to hear it. I want to hear all of it."

A whole host of words tumbled through my mind. Foul, rank words, utterances suitable for porn films or worse. Words I wouldn't have said to him before when we'd talked dirty. But we were older now, life had moved on. We had been through so much together.

As though my inhibitions had become as transparent as the window I was pressed against, I suddenly found it easy to let loose these new words. This was Jacob—I could say anything and it would be okay.

I took a deep breath; surprised by how husky my voice sounded when I started to speak. "Your cock is like a steel rod fucking against my clit. But I want more. I want you to ram it anywhere you want. Take me and do whatever you want with my body, Jacob. I'm yours. What I want doesn't matter—this is all about you and sating your needs."

He grunted, and, although he kept one hand tight on my arse, he slid the other upwards and tangled it in my hair, squashing it between my crown and the glass pane. He pulled me closer, my head and my arse, as if he couldn't get near enough despite the fact that the fronts of our bodies were connected completely.

"Yes, that's it, harder, rougher," I gasped. "Do whatever you want. I'm just a rag doll. I'm here for your pleasure. It doesn't matter what I feel. Hurt me, overpower me, drag me to hell with your most primitive desires and fuck me into oblivion. To a place that's so dark and hot that I won't even remember my own name. You own my cunt, my mouth, my…my arsehole. It's all yours. Fuck me harder, Jacob, so much harder!"

"Jesus fucking Christ," he said, easing his head back to look at my face.

His eyes were wild and flashing; swirling vats of lust. It thrilled me utterly to see something so new and exciting in irises I'd stared into so many times, and knew like the back of my own hand.

"I've got to get inside you, now," he groaned. He bent his knees and shoved his cock deep into my cunt.

I cried out at the forceful stretch of his invasion, but he silenced me with a savage kiss, his open mouth hot and wet and frantic. Against my cheek his breath was hard and fast as he pistoned his hips back and forth. Squeaks from my sweat-damp skin rubbing on the window filled my ears, and I had a fleeting mental image of what my soft, pale body must look like from the outside—my flattened arse pressed to a bloodless white with a big, hairy hand digging into the left cheek and creating dents. My pussy and the dark cleft of my anus exposed and my spine and shoulders shifting with the force of his thrusting…

Gasping for air around our passionate kiss, I locked my hands at his nape. My pussy squeezed him tight, building up to a fantastic orgasm. I remembered how much I enjoyed fucking while we were standing. His rock-hard pubic bone bashed into my clit so perfectly, dragging it upwards with each sublime thrust. Why had we gone for missionary so many times over the last few years when this was so divine? What else had we forgotten that was so good?

"More," he said sharply into my mouth. "Come on, tell me more of what I should do to you, Karen."

I willed my mind to work. It was hard when I was flying high on the thrilling ride to climax, but there was a scenario in my head. Like a seedling bursting through the soil, it stretched to my mouth.

Out it spilled.

"Don't say my name." I gasped as a particularly forceful thrust had his glans stroking my G-spot. "You don't know me. This is a dark alley. I was going home after seeing friends for the evening. A lone lady, vulnerable, heels loud on the cobbles." I paused to heave in a breath, my lungs desperate with the effort of talking as he pounded into me with fervour.

As if sensing my struggle, he slowed his hips but increased the depth of penetration. Every time he was seated to the hilt he jerked, hitting my cervix and reeling my clit into a wondrous state of building pressure.

With a little less air being shunted from my lungs I carried on. My lips touched his neck, just a fraction below his ear, where he smelt masculine and raw and the texture of his skin was smooth but tough. "You saw me, walking into this alley. You were rock-hard for a fuck, so hard, but you were sick of your own hand. Tired of getting yourself off while you looked at porn. So you decided to just take me against my will. It didn't matter that it was me, it could have been any woman, but I happened to be there, that night, when you were feeling hard and brave and desperate. So damn desperate."

"So how did it happen?" he whispered, breathily. He kissed across my cheek and nibbled the shell of my ear, the tempo of his hips a wonderful rhythm that kept my orgasm within reach but also under control. "I need to know. Tell me how we got to this stage. The me-fucking-you stage."

I shut my eyes to the harsh daylight of the room. "I heard your footsteps behind me and turned, scared. When I started to run, you chased me, grabbed me, hauled me against a wall and ripped off my skirt. You were so big and strong and so damn determined." The image in my head was scarily vivid. I could see us wrestling, limbs tangled, and hear the sound of material tearing. Jacob all horny and powerful; me scared and helpless. "You tore off my panties. I screamed for you to get off me, let me go home. But you clamped your hand over my mouth, you didn't care. You wanted me. You wanted to fuck my pretty cunt hard and fast."

Gripping his tense biceps, I built up to that moment of bliss, where climax is inevitable; a beautiful knowledge spreading over me that satiation would soon be mine.

"Ah, love, talk while we come. Keep telling me the story."

I shook, feverish with need now. "You're thrusting into me, your big, bad cock penetrating my pussy, your hands groping my breasts, harsh and cruel. I bite your shoulder. You're furious and twist me to face the wall. My hands flail against sharp brick. The wall is cold and gritty. It smells of damp and rotting food."

"Then what? Tell me, then what?"

"You fuck me from behind." I was almost shouting now, the syllables juddering as his pace increased. "You don't care that I'm not wet for you, you shove into my poor abused pussy over and over. You've still got a hand clamped over my mouth so I can't scream for help and you ride into me like a marauder. I'm overpowered… I'm… Oh, God, Jacob…I'm…going to…"

"Me too, me fucking too."

We came together. It was intense and furious. Our groans and shouts of delight unmuffled and uninhibited.

"Ah, yes, that's it, oh fuck, yes," I cried, actually sinking my teeth into his shoulder.

"Oh, baby, fucking fantastic." He jerked, lodging deep inside me as he spilled his seed high into my body.

My pussy clamped and squeezed him, clit bobbing on his pubic bone, drawing out every last luscious spasm of ecstasy. Suddenly his mouth was on mine again, and he kissed me, deep and profound.

Running my hands over his sweaty shoulders, I clung on, forcing my breasts into the coarse hairs on his chest and battling for breath and sanity.

"Oh, God, that was something else," he said, shuddering within my embrace.

As I slid my palms over his hot back, I was aware that every one of his muscles was taut and tight.

"You made me completely lose it then," he murmured. "I felt like a horny teenager again, doing it for the first time. All control left me."

I giggled breathlessly.

He pulled back and grinned, but kept his cock pumping slowly within me. He looked down. "Ah, fuck, that looks so hot."

I followed his gaze. His veiny, mauve shaft, rising from his black pubic hair, slid backwards and forwards through my paler pubes. It was slick and shiny and still hard and solid. I could just make out the glossy nub of my clit jutting from its hood.

The sight of Jacob entering me was sublime and I would never tire of it. But suddenly I was aware once more of my position against the window, and the memory of the binoculars comment. I went to move my legs from his hips. But he grabbed both my thighs, kept me wrapped tight around him.

"No, don't move. Jesus, I feel like I could come all over again." He looked up and grinned, then ducked for a kiss.

I accepted it happily and a delicious flush of accomplishment filled me. I'd done it. The old Karen was back. I could still talk dirty. I could still make Jacob lose it with words.

But, my goodness, where had those words risen from?

Where on earth had that depraved image of being taken against my will come from? I'd described it so vividly and it had sent me reeling into one damn fine orgasm.

Was there something wrong with me?

Then I realised.

It's the book. That damn filthy book.

Chapter Three

Eventually we separated and I moved away from the window, the glass marked with my sweat and slightly steamy in the corners. I didn't even think to wipe it. Instead, I flopped on the bed, arms and legs spread wantonly as Jacob used the shower first—he knew I'd want time to recover. Besides, the time alone, even if only for five minutes, was needed. I had things to think about—too many things.

Maybe five minutes wouldn't be enough.

Still, I closed my eyes, skin sex-sweat hot, as though I'd caught a fever from our fuck. And I had in a way. Caught a fever that not only burned my skin but seared through me, pushing for more. My throat was dry from sucking in air, and I listened as my pulse slowed and my body returned to normal. Face blazing warmer, I admitted—properly—that talking about that rape scene had given everything we did such an *edge*. Sharp and urgent. Raw and animalistic. It had taken us to a new level, surpassing even the giddy heights our new relationship had been years ago. I never thought we'd get there again, yet here we were.

The wonder of it blew my mind. Clit still aching from such a blissful assault, I surprised myself when my hand glided downwards without my having thought to move it. Hadn't I had enough? Wasn't that orgasm one of the best I'd ever had? Yes, it was, but, my God, I wanted more. I fondled myself, Jacob's sperm thick and warm on my fingers, the smell of it wafting up to swaddle me.

Who would have thought that with age came this…this brand new sexual mountain I was standing on? I'd reached the apex of a new peak and was looking down at the climb.

We'd fucked against a window, and despite my Peeping Tom worries, I could also admit it turned me on to think of someone seeing us. And me saying my fantasy out loud, Jacob being turned on by it too. Now there was a revelation. My man, who abhorred violence of any kind towards a woman, had been turned on by the thought of forced entry.

And then the thought came, one I didn't want to entertain, but it was there, bold and bright just the same.

Was there something wrong with *both* of us?

Rape was a vile crime. An act that was evil and depraved and should be punished with castration and life in prison at the very least. But, of course, I didn't really want to be raped. I just wanted my loving husband to fuck me within an aggressive sexual fantasy.

Jacob entering the room after his shower prevented me pondering any further on that question. He smiled at me, white towel secure around his middle, using another to dry his hair. Relaxed, that was how he looked, like this weekend had been the key to unlocking the door that had held tension inside him, giving it the freedom to leave his body. I had something to do with that. Me, with my lurid fantasy that had appealed to him so much too.

Inordinately proud of myself, I got off the bed, sly smile of my own stretching wide, and breezed past him and into the bathroom without a word. I didn't want to discuss it, wanted a little more time to let a new seed of an idea, which had always been there but hadn't been watered, begin to grow.

The shower water pattered over me, a soft caress that left me refreshed and raring to go. The glass walls of the cubicle clouded, giving me the sense that I was completely alone, and my sinful idea began to bloom. I realised, if what I had in mind was going to work, that we had things to do before nightfall—important things. Like visiting the shops so I could buy a new outfit and high heels, clothes I wouldn't usually wear. Nothing slutty, just different from my usual jeans, T-shirts and sturdy boots.

I wondered, as I soaped my hair and body, what those clothes would feel like. For too long I'd chosen safe items—jeans; long, baggy T-shirts; sweaters that covered my arse and hid the fact that beneath them I actually had some shape. I supposed that the extra weight had made me self-conscious and I'd hidden my body's imperfections. Or what I saw as imperfections. Since I'd had the girls, Jacob had encouraged me to sod what anyone else thought and wear what I wanted, but I'd pointed out that a muffin top wasn't something I wanted to advertise. I didn't care that most other women I knew had them, I just... God, I just wished *I* didn't have one.

I glanced down at myself. Naked, I didn't look too bad. Maybe if I bought clothes that fitted properly I wouldn't have a problem. And there was that TV programme, wasn't there? The one where those two women told the viewer which clothes suited which body. Yes, that was it. I'd buy some new clothes—as well as the ones needed for tonight—and see if they stopped me from feeling like such a blob.

I diverted my thoughts back to the ones that demanded my immediate attention. We needed to check out the streets around the hotel, see if we could find somewhere suitable. Somewhere quiet and dark and seedy.

Out of the shower, I wrapped a towel around my body and secured it beneath my armpits. I left the bathroom dressed the same way Jacob had, but with an extra towel twisted around my hair.

He turned from the window to look at me, jeans moulded to his legs, a casual light blue shirt yet to be buttoned giving me an exciting glimpse of his bare chest and a tuft of armpit hair where the fabric flapped open. Had he been staring through the glass, remembering our encounter? Had it got him thinking of the same thing as me—acting it out tonight?

"You all right, love?" he asked, voice back to its usual steady tone.

"Yes. You?" Sudden shyness washed over me. A nugget of anger vibrated in my belly at that. I wasn't going to allow myself to go back to how I was. Not now. Not when I had something so *bad* on the agenda. I straightened my shoulders and tugged the towel from my hair. Stared right at him, a woman with a sexy mission in mind. I'd take control, make things happen. Show him we still *had* it. "We need to go out. I have to buy a few things."

"Things?" He walked over to me and weaved his fingers in my damp, tangled hair.

But I wanted him to jam them there, to fist my hair and yank my head back, pull until it hurt. The thought grew, took shape, showing images in my head that I perhaps should have been ashamed of.

"Am I weird?" I asked. "Weird and wrong to want...what I said I wanted?"

He smiled again, cocked his head, and stroked through my hair.

Yank it, damn it!

"If you're weird, then I'm weird."

His shrug said it all. There was nothing to worry about. So long as we were both happy with it, then what was the harm?

"Good." I reached up to take his wrist, bringing his hand down so he cupped my cheek. The startling vision of him slapping it shocked me. Did I want to go *that* far? Have the fantasy so *real?* "Then you won't mind acting out what I told you earlier, will you." Statement. Asking it as a question gave him the option to refuse.

He widened his eyes, unable to hide his surprise quickly enough.

So he hadn't been thinking the same as me when he'd stared out of the window, then.

After clearing his throat, he said, "For real?" He glanced around the room. "It's hardly big enough in here to act it out, love, but we'll give it a go."

I laughed, a throaty sound that hadn't belonged to me in years. "Not in here, Jacob. Fuck, no. I want you to 'rape' me outside. Down an alley."

* * * *

I wobbled a little in the black stiletto heels, and the cold air on my bare legs wasn't something I'd bargained for. Stares from passers-by as I did my best to strut seductively down the darkened street weren't something I'd banked on either. It had been too long since someone other than Jacob had looked at me in *that* way. Too long since I'd worn a short black skirt that left nothing to the imagination and a cute red top that did the same. I'd applied makeup, too, taken more care than just the usual blast of the dryer to style my hair, and a sense of being *me, myself,* of being 'a woman' had given me a more confident stride.

In our room, Jacob had whistled when I'd presented myself to him, said my blonde hair looked damn hot and sexy against the red top. I'd felt so pleased with myself, having bought clothes that fitted well and highlighted my curves in a seductive way.

I glanced back. Jacob followed, maybe a hundred metres away, also in new clothing. Black jeans, black bomber jacket, beanie hat covering his hair. A beanie hat that, when he pulled down the folded cuff, became a ski mask. God, my stomach had clenched with excitement when I'd spotted it earlier. The thought of being taken by a rough-and-ready masked man had wet my slit right there in the shop. I'd looked at him, mask in my hand, thumb brushing the wool, and he'd nodded and walked away. If he hadn't, would he have grabbed hold of me and done something he shouldn't have?

I liked that—it gave me power to know I affected him so much. Bizarre really, when it was having power taken away from me that ruled my thoughts.

Smiling now, I turned away from him and faced ahead, concentrating on putting one foot in front of the other without my heels catching in the gaps between the uneven slabs of the path. It was weird walking in these shoes after so many years of flats or trainers. I'd worn heels on occasion, to weddings and parties, but the last time had been so long ago it was like learning to totter in them all over again.

Our first stop hogged the corner across the road, a squat, old-fashioned red-brick building, the dark green swinging sign proclaiming it as Brewer's Droop. I'd laughed at that earlier, told Jacob if he thought of having more than one drink in there tonight he'd better not prove the pub name true.

I needed him hard and more than able to carry out the plans I'd whispered in his ear. As I'd stood with him, wrapped in that towel, I'd given him every delicious detail, then pulled back and studied him, checked whether he really was up for it and not just agreeing to indulge me. From the flush of his cheeks and the gleam in his eye I could tell he was willing. He'd pulled me closer, kissed me hard, his cock growing by the second. If I hadn't pulled away we would never have left that room.

My steps were taking me closer to the pub, so I crossed the road, hips swaying, heels tapping the asphalt. Once I was on the other side, I glanced back again, so giddy with excitement I couldn't have described it if I'd tried. Jacob had crossed over too; he was looking menacing in the doorway of the tool shop we'd visited that afternoon. Yes, I wanted this fantasy to be as realistic as possible and the purchase we'd made there would see to that.

Shadows embraced his right side so he appeared to be half a person in the illumination of the orange-hued streetlamp. He looked sinister, like a man lying in wait, a predator ready to pounce on his prey. I wondered what he was thinking as he stared back at me, whether he saw me as his wife or was getting into his role, seeing me as an object and not a person, the one thing he wanted that would sate his desires and make him feel whole. I hoped he thought the latter. I wanted him to be so unlike his usual self that I would fail to recognise him.

Getting well into my own role, I narrowed my eyes at him, as though I wondered why he'd tailed me, and waited for his reaction. It came as a scowl and a nasty sneer on his lips designed to frighten but instead it gave me a thrill to think of him being someone he wasn't—violent and mean, ruthless and without conscience.

Fuck, I was getting wet.

I frowned, shaping my mouth into a suitable grimace, and turned away. At the pub door, dark green with brass handles and opaque windows, I took a deep breath and quickly entered, as if seeking the safety of other people. The scent of stale beer beneath that of the freshly poured pints assaulted me, and it took a few breaths before the aroma went away. Other smells took over—too many aftershaves and perfumes, hairsprays and deodorants from the hundred or so people standing or sitting around—and I breathed through my mouth to combat the overwhelming smell. Music blared from hidden speakers, some modern tune I'd heard on the radio last week, and I felt so alive, so *with it,* that I almost gave a beaming smile. Another frisson of excitement plundered through me, my belly clenching and a bubble of expectancy waiting to pop in my throat.

It was happening. The fantasy that had been hidden within the pages of a shamefully dirty book was becoming my reality.

I ignored lurid glances from a group of men who lounged at one corner of the bar, their stares giving me an unexpected boost of confidence. I was still desirable, still worth a look, and for a moment I felt foolish for being so pleased about that. A brief thought of them coming over and asking if I wanted a drink brought a shudder of revulsion, though. Since I'd met Jacob, other men just hadn't entered my mind. Besides, they wouldn't approach me, I knew that. I was just being fanciful.

One of the barmen, an aged fellow with tufts of coarse grey hair at his temples and none on his shiny head, took my order for a large glass of white wine, a denture-ridden smile transforming his wrinkled face. I wondered what he saw every night and what he thought about it. People meeting for illicit trysts. Obvious extra-marital affairs. Drunk men gaining bravado from alcohol, trying to pull women so obviously out of their league. Women, legs like elastic from too many alcopops, hoping their knight in shining armour would notice them and sweep them off their feet.

I had my knight. I had my castle. I just wanted a little enhancement.

The barman turned away and walked to the wine cooler, getting in the way of another, much younger man who bustled around getting drinks for a gaggle of twenty-something women down at the other end. They shrieked at a joke one of them had told, and I recalled nights I'd spent out with the girls in my university days.

I didn't miss them.

I returned my attention to the old man, and as he poured I took in my surroundings, wondering where Jacob was. He'd hidden himself well, then, would watch me as planned until my drink was nearly gone and then he'd show himself.

The wine, when I took a gulp, was cold and crisp on my tongue and gave me something to do while I threw surreptitious glances about the place. The men on the corner leered some more, but rather than please me this time it made me a little uneasy. Jacob still wasn't in plain sight, and I could only hope he was watching them, keeping an eye on the situation. One of them stared a bit too hard for a bit too long, and as a blush crept into my cheeks, I turned away.

My glass of wine had suddenly become an interesting study.

I sipped, awareness of being watched prickling my skin. It wasn't meant to be the eyes of other men—only Jacob—and the unpredictability of my plan, the thought of it going wrong, hadn't entered my head until now.

Wine almost gone, I searched the pub with my gaze for

the one man who mattered and finally spotted him standing behind the crowd of men at the corner. He glared through the space between a black-haired beefcake and a blond wiry guy, his face hard, mouth set in a grim line.

The game was on.

I tossed the remainder of my drink down my throat and left the pub, the shock of cool air adding to the buzz of adventure shuddering through me. A few metres ahead lay the dead-end alley between two buildings we'd agreed on, and I checked behind me so the next act could begin.

Jacob wasn't there.

Come on! Where are you?

I slowed, head bent, and wondered why he'd deviated from the plan. He was supposed to be right behind me, making it clear he *had* been tailing me since we'd left the hotel. I was meant to make my mouth into an 'O' of shock, whimper, and rush down the alley to get away from him.

A quick flash of footsteps sounded behind me, and I smiled, keeping my head down. So *this* was how he wanted it, was it? *He* wanted to control this fantasy. Fine, I'd let him, but he'd better be good!

At the alley entrance, I rested my hand on the brick and made to turn around, to give him that little mewl of fright, but a hand clamped over my mouth before I had the chance. I was jerked backwards against a very male chest and held tight by a strong, thick arm across my belly. I lost purchase in my damn heels and stumbled. I bit back a squeal, my hands flailing as I instinctually fought for balance even though Jacob was holding me steady.

"Down here," a voice said.

A voice that wasn't Jacob's.

Oh, shit. No, this couldn't be happening. Not for real.

Bone-cold terror coursed through my veins, turning my blood to ice. I lashed out, arms flapping, raising them in order to smack the bastard and cause him pain, make him lose his grip. He held me tighter. I jabbed my arse back, hoping to catch him in the groin where it would hurt the most, but my efforts were wasted.

Oh, God. Where the fucking hell is Jacob?

I struggled, fighting to break free, trying to scream and failing. That hand prevented any sound escaping. Shunted down the alley, the man's hold firm and growing stronger, I frantically brought my hands up with the intent of scratching his face or gouging at his eyes. More footsteps sounded, sure, quick strides; loud taps that struck the alley floor in time with my heartbeat. Flashes of the men at the bar whipped through my mind, and I imprinted them there for when I would need to recall them for the police. It had to be them. At least the man who had stared the most.

My wrists were caught in front of me by another set of hands.

Fuck. Are they all *here?*

My knees weakened, unable to give my legs the strength to hold me upright, and, weirdly, the thought of those young women with alcohol-heavy legs sprang to mind. Why the hell did that come into my head when I was... when I was being...?

I was roughly carried further down the alley into the dark shadows beyond. The smell of weathered brick didn't seem as delicious as it had a few hours ago when we'd checked out our locations. It was ugly, searing the inside of my nostrils, and a smell I'd never forget; branded in my mind as a memory I'd rather not have.

How quickly fate could change the best-laid plans. And to think this had all been for some dirty kink. Now the truly awful crime was about to be inflicted upon me. How foolish and naïve we'd been. Having a fantasy about it was one thing, but having it happen for real was an entirely different ballgame.

The man holding my face and body let go, and I grabbed a breath in order to scream. Whoever held my wrists had better get ready to run, because I wasn't being taken against my will like this.

Wriggling, I faced the looming silhouette, who drew my

arms down and held my wrists in one hand. Before the scream could emerge, he steered me towards the wall of a building so fast my mind couldn't keep up. He slammed me against the brick, and the air I would have used to scream gusted out of my mouth. I snatched another breath, ready to try again, but he pressed his palm over my lips. I couldn't see him – the darkness was absolute and the sound of receding footsteps made me glance to the alley opening. A man disappeared around the corner onto the street, leaving me trapped with some bastard who was squeezing my wrists rhythmically and was breathing too heavy. Had those men in the pub got hold of Jacob? Thoughts for my own safety fled, replaced by fear that my husband was being beaten up by thugs.

One of them was here, pressing himself against me, one knee prising my legs apart. Fuck, no. He wasn't touching me like that. Who did he think he was?

I bucked, jerking ineffectively against his hold. He was too strong, too fucking strong, but I'd keep fighting, keep trying to get him off me if it was the last thing I did.

"You like this, bitch? Eh? You like my buddy grabbing you for me?"

Confusion rippled through me, chasing the terror away. *Jacob?*

He let go of my wrists, jammed his fingers in my hair and wound it around them. And yanked.

Juices flooded my pussy.

I raised my hands, pushing them between us to reach his face, fingertips meeting with wool, the ridge of an eyehole, then skin. I traced over that tiny bit of exposed face in search of the little knot of raised scar tissue that should be there if this really was Jacob.

It was there, beside his eye. Relief ploughed through me, leaving me a sagging, weak mess. I wanted to give in and cry, to let out the rest of the extreme tension that had consumed me, to rail at him for changing our plan and frightening me shitless. But he had other ideas.

"Yeah, you fucking loved it, didn't you, bitch? And you want me fucking you now, hard and fast, the wall gritty on your bare arse after I've ripped your knickers off. Bet you're wet. So wet that my cock'll slip inside you so fast you won't have time to catch your breath."

Jacob had turned into someone I'd wanted him to be for so long. Sensations, so many of them—shock, surprise, pleasure—overcame me, and for the first time since he'd spoken, my clit swelled. The throb there grew as I sensed him staring at me, the heat from his ragged breaths fanning my face.

"You'd answer, wouldn't you? Except I won't let you. My hand's staying where it is for now, you damn filthy whore. Clamped over your pretty little mouth. Bet that mouth can suck cock good. Bet those lips and tongue can make a man come hard. Yeah, my hand's staying put. Don't want you screaming. Not that kind of scream, anyway."

He lifted his knee, settling it at my crotch, and moved it back and forth. My skirt rose with each movement, the air cold on my newly exposed skin. His jeans abraded my clit through my gusset, rough, pleasing strokes that fuelled the kernel of desire into something bigger, more intense.

He'd got some guy to join our game, how I didn't know, but right now I didn't care.

I wanted a fuck, a rough-as-hell fuck.

And I was going to get it.

Chapter Four

Jacob kept one hand clamped over my mouth as the other roamed my body. I pushed and shoved at his arms and chest. Fighting my attacker, I wriggled and writhed to be free. But my efforts were futile—he was so strong and determined. I was a lamb against a lion.

He cupped my breasts, his hands rough and frantic, squeezing first one then the other, leaving them pulsing points of pain. It was not how he normally touched me—there was no respect there, no consideration or tenderness.

"I'm gonna fuck you like you've never been fucked before, bitch. I bet you've never had a real man like me, have you, eh? Just a bunch of losers who couldn't get it up, I bet."

"Mmmph," I whimpered behind his palm.

He grunted and fumbled with his fly button. I couldn't see, but I knew his cock would be freed instantly. He'd gone without boxers—didn't want the extra barrier, he'd said.

He gave a deft flick of his wrist and shoved my tiny Lycra skirt upwards, its flimsiness no protection from this masked man hell-bent on fucking me. There was a ripping sound as he tore my panties from my body, and I was vaguely aware of the burning sensation the taut fabric had left on my skin. There would be a bruised, red mark tomorrow.

And I would be proud of it.

Jacob breathed heavily, the noise of the air rushing in and out of his lungs rasping through the mask, down onto my face. He didn't wear his usual spiced aftershave. He just smelt of raw man—heated arousal and dingy desires. It made him all the sexier—if that were possible.

"Open your pussy, whore."

I shook my head, mumbled, "No", and sped up my squirming.

In response he stooped, hooked his forearm behind my knee, and hoisted my right leg into the air. My hip joint clicked in complaint, but I barely noticed its awkward position. All I could think of was how vulnerable he'd made my pussy.

He wasted no time in taking advantage. Pinning me to the wall with his solid chest, he shoved his thick cock into my folds. He missed and the blunt head stabbed my delicate flesh. I screwed up my eyes and groaned in discomfort. He ignored me. Repositioned and rammed forwards again.

This time his aim was accurate, and he slid high and fast into my sopping pussy. I tried to cry out as my channel struggled to accommodate him. So many times he'd fucked me; countless times, but still I'd always had the sublime stretching sensation whenever he rode to the hilt on his first stroke. It was a combination of pain and pleasure, and I lapped it up, wishing the erotic bite would last longer.

"Yeah, bitch, take it," he grunted. "Take all of my big, hard cock. It's the best one you've ever fucking had."

He withdrew and rushed back in, pounding against my clit with his hair-fuzzed pubis.

It felt divine.

"You were asking for it tonight in these slutty clothes," he hissed by my ear. "Short, *fuck me* skirt and top so tight your tits were practically on show. I could see your whorish nipples poking through. They want to be bitten hard, don't they?"

His vulgar language thrilled me utterly, but I wished he'd let go of my mouth. Breathless and claustrophobic, twisting my head, I tried to shake him off, but he didn't let up his grip.

"This is not about your pleasure or what you want," he snarled, increasing the grip and his fingertips pressing into my cheeks like pincers. "You're mine. I'm fucking you how *I* want to. This is all about me. I've taken your body to do whatever I please with."

I whimpered and balled my fists into his bomber jacket. Tugged hard, trying to get his attention.

But he ignored me and buried his head in my neck. He grabbed my left breast and pinched my nipple roughly through my top as he steamed in and out of my cunt. There was no consideration for me at all. It was the opposite end of the spectrum to kind, gentle Jacob, and I really did feel like he was another person. I was being screwed by a darkly twisted stranger in a dirty alley.

The whole situation and Jacob's carnal, uninhibited hunger combined with his enthusiastic acting skills sent fiery fingers of exquisite pleasure sizzling over my skin. This was what I'd asked for and, as always, wonderful Jacob was giving it to me.

With each shunt his breathing quickened and his bodyweight pressing into me increased. I was helpless. He was in control one hundred per cent. I couldn't even verbalise what I wanted or needed. If I'd wanted it to stop, which I absolutely didn't, I couldn't have done anything about it. I was on for the ride—the whole ride.

Just as I thought Jacob was getting ready to come—the giveaway signs of his hips arching tightly and his groaning becoming erratic—he withdrew and spun me to face the wall. He barely lifted his hand from my mouth before it slammed back down so there was no time to speak or scream or hardly even drag in a decent breath.

"Now you're really going to take it," he growled into my ear, his voice possessed, demented. It was an octave lower than normal, and the sharp woollen mask muffled it, making it seem even more unfamiliar and dangerous.

Excitement mixed with the shock of our situation as I remembered the next part of my fantasy. Now he would take my pussy from behind. It had been so long since we'd done it like that—and standing, who knew when?

Again I shook my head. I was the frantic victim. This time my right temple banged and scratched on the gritty surface of the wall. Trying to cry out, pulling rank air in through my nose. My spine jerked as he kicked my legs apart with his feet, not caring if he bruised my ankles.

God, this was getting deliciously rough.

He nudged his cock down the cleft of my buttocks until the head sat at my anus. He was wide and greedy and probed with a scary determination.

Instinct caused me to thrust away, but I couldn't go far. I was held too tightly against the brickwork.

He let out a nasty chuckle. "I can do that if I want to, bitch."

My lust-addled brain fogged with confusion. *That* hadn't been part of the plan. What was he talking about? Jacob had never fucked my arse, ever, and if he was going to, wouldn't we need lube?

"If my cock wants to stab into your arse then it can," he growled. "You're mine to do whatever the fuck I want with, remember that. You have no say in it, none whatsoever."

He exerted more pressure. My tight ring clamped, and a tremor of anxiety rattled up my spine. I couldn't cope with this. Not now, not here. But if he pressed much harder he would pop into me. And it would hurt—it would hurt like crazy. He was so thick and impossibly wide.

I wanted to scream, to get away. For the second time I wondered just what trouble I'd invited with my dangerous fantasy. Because he was right. He had absolute control over me, and there was nothing in the world I could do about it if he decided to ram into my virginal hole and fuck me in the most primitive of ways.

"But lucky for you I want to fuck your pussy," he said, sliding his cock further into my folds. "So brace yourself for it, whore, I'm going to take whatever you can offer and then some more."

He rode to the hilt again. My slick pussy welcomed him this time, and my G-spot roared awake as his ridged glans smoothed over it.

"Ah, fuck, you're so hot and wet," he groaned in a

pleasure-soaked voice.

I tipped my head back and arched my spine, tilted my pelvis so he hit my sweet point just right. A strangled moan of delight bled from my lips. The angle was perfect—Heaven and Paradise and Nirvana all mixed into one.

"You like being taken roughly in a filthy dark alley?" he asked, his voice mean again, back in character. "You like being taken by a sick pervert, don't you? You're such a foul slut, this is what you deserve."

I tried to shake my head, reach behind myself to pull and punch him. But it was no good. With each thrust I was being sent skyward, and I forgot that I was supposed to be trying to escape.

His pounding gained speed, as though he was racing an invisible opponent and dragging me with him.

Ecstasy was knocking on my door.

"Ah, fuck yes, yes..."

I recognised the sounds of Jacob reaching the point of no return and surrendered to my own orgasm. It was right there. Blinding lights flashed through the darkness as I embraced a deep, profoundly satisfying G-spot climax. The first one from this internal hot point in so, so long. As it swept through me a long, tortured groan ripped from my chest and gurgled in my throat.

"Ah, yes, squeeze me like that, bitch," he said in a strained voice. "Just like that, whore."

His foul language extended my climax, and I was still throbbing as his seed spurted into me. Copious and viscous, it heated my core. Pleasure had overridden sanity, and Jacob had tunnelled into a dark part of my soul that I hadn't even known was there.

He stilled.

Landing from my high, I became aware of my chest and bare legs, which were now bashed up against the damp, cool wall, my head also pressed into it as Jacob's weight leaned heavily into me.

I twisted in discomfort, scratching my forearms on the

pock-marked bricks. Quickly, he withdrew and lifted his body, but kept his hand tight over my mouth.

"Now, you're gonna have to keep quiet while I take off," he whispered harshly. "Cause if you've got plans on screaming, I'll be straight back to strangle that sweet fucking throat of yours." He snorted unpleasantly. "Got it?"

Nodding, because this was all part of the plan, I felt a thick trickle run down my inner thigh. Warm and heavy, it seeped almost to my knee. I could just imagine what the milky gloop looked like. I was in one hell of a fucked-up state.

It was perfect.

"Good," he said, "so keep it quiet." Finally, he took his hand from my face.

"Oi, what's going on down there?"

The sudden shout at the end of the alley grabbed our attention.

Not part of the plan.

Jacob's body heat left me completely, and I spun to see him shoving his semi-hard cock into his jeans. With a quick tug he removed the ski mask, the action spiking his damp hair upright.

Yanking down my skirt with one hand, I reached for his with my other. Entwined our fingers and squeezed away the worried words he knew I wanted to say. My heart thudded and my stomach clenched. I was scared. We'd been caught playing our lurid, sick game. But by whom?

A torchlight flickered over us, and I blinked rapidly.

"What the hell?" The silhouette of a tall, broad man came into view at the end of the alley. He walked towards us, his face in darkness, but his purposeful stride told me to be wary. I could only imagine what we must look like—me tarty, messed up and still panting hard from my climax, and Jacob all big and menacing, also breathing heavily. It wouldn't take a genius to guess what we'd been up to. But if he thought it had been rape, anything could happen.

He might even be a copper. Shit!

"Nothing's going on," Jacob said, tightening his grip on my fingers and pulling me towards the approaching figure.

"Looks like something to me." The voice was northern and deep, confident and assertive.

Jacob bent his head to mine. "Can you run?"

"I…I don't know."

Run? My legs felt like jelly, and I'd already exerted myself considerably. My heart rate hadn't recovered from that.

"Try, love, you're gonna have to try."

And with that he darted forward, tugging my hand, leaving me no choice but to run behind him. My shoes were unforgiving, but adrenaline spurred me on and I banged one foot down in front of the other, praying my ankles wouldn't turn. The cum on my thigh cooled and the night air washed over my naked pussy, only just hidden by my perilously short skirt.

"Hey," the man shouted, shining the torch into my face as we passed. "Wait."

"Sorry," I panted, pressing a hand against my jiggling breasts.

"Missy, are you all right?"

"Yes, I'm fine, absolutely fine," I said. Then, as we reached the road, I threw over my shoulder in a light, jovial voice, "In fact, I've never been better."

Chapter Five

We ran through the town, Jacob still clutching my hand, a breathy bout of laughter exploding from me. People stared, but so what? I didn't care. It was as though something inside me had been released, a new beginning, a new phase of myself that I hoped would keep growing. Exploring our sex life from now on would be exciting. After all, I'd told my husband one of my deepest desires and he'd accepted it, helped to play it out. What was the harm in telling him the others? If he didn't want to go there, that was fine, but if I didn't ask, I'd never know, would I? Again a memory of the book came to my mind. Me flicking through its dusty pages and being both shocked and turned on as each chapter revealed its sinfully sexy fantasies. Each idea embedding itself into my subconscious, burying deep until the time was right. Was that time now?

My ankle threatened to turn and I forced illicit scenarios from my thoughts and concentrated on where my footsteps were landing. A quick glance behind ensured that the man hadn't followed, so I slowed, taking my hand from Jacob's so I could remove those bloody heels. I carried them in one hand while slipping my other through the crook of his arm and, feeling gloriously breathless, I looked at him.

His eyes sparkled, the kind of twinkle I hadn't seen in such a long time, and a smile hooked up one corner of his mouth. His cheeks were flushed despite the nip in the air and he gave a low chuckle.

"Good, wasn't it?" he asked, eyeing me with a look that dared me to respond in the negative.

"Fucking wonderful!" And I meant it. Yes, his hand

over my mouth for an extended period wasn't something I wanted to repeat, and I'd have to speak to him about that, fine-tune the details for next time, but otherwise… It *had* been wonderful. Exactly what I'd wanted, scratches, marks and all.

"That guy…" He shrugged, like the action would make us being caught go away. "Wonder who he was, what he thought?"

"I don't give a shit. I'm on a high." As we walked on, a sudden thought hit me. "Hey, what happened to the hammer we bought in the tool shop?"

He glanced my way again. "Shit! I forgot about that. I was so excited…"

"Did you even bring it with you?"

"No, left it in our room."

"There'll be other times. That handle…"

Lapsing into silence, we continued our walk to the hotel, and I was sure he was as lost in thoughts of what we'd just done as I was. The whole episode, from Jacob getting that guy to join in, to the fuck itself, and then that man finding us, had been more than I'd expected. I'd ask him later about how he'd convinced someone to join in our game. Whether he'd paid him to do it.

How had we gone so long without experimenting like this? Age *must* have something to do with it; maturity had brought a different perspective on what was right and wrong. Was any of it wrong? I didn't care if some thought it was.

It was right for us.

In the hotel lobby, all potted palms scattered among carefully positioned chairs and low coffee tables, my bare feet slapped on the cold marble floor. A porter, pushing an empty suitcase trolley, gave me the once-over, his perusal ending at my pink-painted toenails. He frowned as though my sort didn't belong in this hotel, and that brought on another rush of laughter.

"What's so funny?" Jacob asked, leading me towards the

lift.

"Him looking at me." I nodded at the porter, who glanced back over his shoulder and shook his close-cropped head. "Me with no shoes on. Dressed like a tart."

Jacob leaned across to whisper, "Ah, you're a trashy whore, that's what he's thinking, bitch."

His voice—that tone—set me off again. My stomach churned as excitement stirred and my knees weakened. I knew I would be ready for more fucking once we got to our room.

And we did. Fucked the rest of the weekend away, cramming every spare moment we had into being with one another. We didn't make it to the art gallery, didn't take the time to wander the streets and take in our environment. The bedroom was the only sight we needed. That and each other.

I had yet to tell Jacob of my other erotic fantasies, but I needed to think about them myself first. See if I really wanted to allow the contents of that book to grip me again before inviting him to join in. Besides, rolling them around in my mind and testing how they made me feel was all part of the arousal. The build-up to confessing what I wanted was frightening yet exhilarating.

And the actual playing it out was the icing on the damn cake.

* * * *

Thoughts of being fucked in the arse had begun to intrude on a regular basis since we'd returned home. I'd had no idea Jacob wanted that until our time in the alley, and I found myself pondering what it would feel like more often than I cared to admit. With Jacob away for the weekend—his turn on the rota for a work seminar he'd rather not have to attend—and the girls staying with his mum and dad, I had nothing much to do *but* think. I cleaned until the house sparkled, read until my eyes crossed and lay awake at night, my mind wandering to how it would feel to have Jacob's cock inside my arse. And the more I thought about it, the more it appealed. The more I thought about it, the more I knew we would do it.

I imagined it would hurt at first, having an alien object inside *that* hole. When browsing internet sites on the subject—yes, I'd been curious enough for that—the general consensus was that the pain turned pleasurable after a while. I could cope with that, and I guessed Jacob could too, considering he'd been close to fucking me in that spot in that alley.

Had he been thinking of it for a long time and just hadn't said? I'd hidden my rape fantasy from him because I hadn't wanted him to think me perverted or weird. Had he done the same with anal sex? I hated the thought of him feeling unable to share everything with me, and for the first time I realised he may well have felt the same about my recent revelation. That I hadn't trusted him enough to share.

I sighed and flopped onto our bed, staring out of the window at the onset of night. Funny, but I noticed how much the layout of our room resembled the one at the hotel, only our furniture was real wood and the walls were bright with sunny yellow paint and gold-coloured bedding. The cream curtains fluttered in the slight breeze, sifting through the open crack, cooling the room to a pleasant temperature. I needed it—I'd been getting far too hot lately. And I also needed Jacob to call. I wanted to hear his voice, and I was just about ready to fully confess my latest fantasy. With me here all alone, we could talk without interruption. I hated being away from him like this, and who knew, a bit of phone sex might bring us closer, despite the miles separating us.

I idled away the time conjuring images of Jacob holding me close, my back to his chest, his cock nudging my arse cleft. I imagined how his rigid tip would butt my puckered hole, trying to gain entrance, his hands spanning my hips as he held me steady.

"Bend over, bitch," he'd say.

And I'd obey, perhaps clutching the windowsill, perhaps the footrest, or maybe even the headboard as we both knelt on the bed. The locations weren't my main focus, though. The entry was.

My cunt clenched and juices seeped, my clit starting that delicious throb that told me I'd need to masturbate to relieve it. Jacob had to call soon or I'd begin without him. Again the image of his cock in my arse appeared, and I reached over to my bedside cabinet, feeling guilty at knowing what I was about to do.

I was going to explore by myself before telling him what I wanted.

Finding the small blue butt plug I'd bought over the internet and the lube that had gained me a puzzled look from the supermarket cashier as she'd swiped it over the barcode reader, I began the task of preparing my arse for invasion. Squeezing a glob of lube onto my finger, I lay back and opened my legs wide, bringing my knees up and my heels close to my body. The position was so rude, so exposed; lying there on our bed with the curtains fluttering in the breeze. Thank goodness neighbours couldn't see in.

I reached down, fingertips brushing my clit before seeking out my arsehole. I found it, and tested its resistance as I pushed against it. The tip of my finger popped through, and the tight clench of the rim around it hadn't been something I was expecting. With a gentle movement, I eased my finger in further, experiencing the sensation of needing to go to the toilet. This hadn't been something I'd anticipated either, and I kept still for a moment, wondering if I really needed to go or whether it was just my body's initial reaction.

It seemed the latter was the case and as the feeling subsided I was able to insert a little more of my finger. The entry passage was rigid, unyielding, and I wondered how the hell Jacob's cock would fit inside. Already my rim was burning; the slight stretch a tad painful.

What had I been thinking, wanting this?

The lure of that burn, that pain turning into pleasure, spurred me on, though. If I didn't like it, I wouldn't ask Jacob if he wanted to try it. I removed my finger, although it still felt as if it was in there, and lubed the butt plug. This was bigger than my finger, wider and longer too, with a pointed end that should glide in easily. It did, but not without the burn, and the lube exacerbated it, made it feel like my arsehole was on fire.

An inch-wide toy did that? Jacob's cock was far broader.

I was in a whole heap of a completely different type of trouble with this fantasy.

Gritting my teeth in anticipation of pain, I eased the plug up and down. A strange sensation of my arse being filled and the plug rubbing against the wall separating it from my cunt took my thoughts on a different journey.

How would it feel to have my arse *and* pussy filled?

Using the fingers of my free hand, I inserted them into my other hole, pushing in and out in time with the butt plug. I pressed against the wall, feeling the rigidity of the plug, the sponginess of my arousal. And then the phone rang.

I took my fingers from my pussy and jabbed the speakerphone button.

"Hello?"

"Hi, love, how are you?"

"Fine," I managed, my throat tight.

"And the girls?"

I struggled to keep lust from my voice as I sent my hands back down between my spread-eagled legs. "Er, yep, good. I spoke to them earlier."

"I'm sorry I'm ringing so late, it's been a heck of an intense day. I've only just got back to my hotel room."

"That's okay, I..." My voice trailed off as I subjected the plug to another prod and it popped completely in for the first time. I blew out a long, slow breath, willing for control of my body as wicked sensations ruled.

"What are you doing?" he asked.

"I'm…I'm just lying on the bed." I squirmed, the fullness overwhelming and my anus taut and hot. It didn't matter where I wriggled, though, the feeling followed.

"Are you thinking of me?"

"God, yes, yes, Jacob. I wish you were here. I wish you were here being the man you were in the alley. It was so hot, so shocking." My words were fast and tripped over themselves.

He hesitated for a second, then lowered his voice. "I can be him again if you want?"

"Now?"

"Yes, now, if that's what you want."

A fevered flush of anticipation travelled over my skin, and my pelvis contracted around the invasion in my arse. I wanted Jacob to be that primitive, carnal man who took what he wanted. The thought of him speaking like that while I was so aroused and rudely penetrated was divine.

There was a moment of suspended, silent anticipation. I could hear him breathing.

"Are you touching yourself, you filthy little whore?" Jacob's raw, rusty rapist's voice shimmered through me, bringing a tide of emotions with it.

My breath hitched and I shut my eyes. "Yes."

"Naked?"

"Yes."

"Are you wet for the evil, depraved man you shouldn't want but do?"

"Very."

"You really are a slut, aren't you, always asking for it."

"I'm asking, I'm asking for all of it. I want the man who grabbed me in the alley and fucked me against the wall until I could barely remember my own name. I want that man to take me again, hard and fast and without a thought for me, just himself."

His breath hitched, and the sound of it brought a spear of pleasure to my cunt. I drove two fingers back into my wet heat.

"Tell me exactly what you've been doing to your slutty little body while you've been thinking of that sick fuck."

Did I want to do that? Be totally honest about what I'd been doing? I couldn't make up my mind, and my mouth engaged before I could stop it. "I have a butt plug in my arse."

"Fuck. Christ, Karen."

I gave a strained smile at catching him off guard. Of shaking him out of character. He hadn't expected a response like that. We hadn't had phone sex in years.

"What does it feel like? Tell me…whore."

The last word was a tag-on, broken in half, and came out croaky. I could imagine him sitting on the edge of the bed, shoulders tense, fists balled as the image of me bombarded his mind. His added responsibility of staying in role, drooping his neck and causing him to gnaw on the inside of his cheek the way he did when concentrating.

"It stings, but I like it."

"More. Tell me more."

"I have my fingers in my pussy, too. I'm imagining a vibrator in there and your cock in my arse. You fucking me until I scream." There, I'd said it.

"Oh, God." His tone was throttled with lust.

"Close your eyes, Jacob. I want you to imagine it. Picture me finger-fucking my cunt and moving the butt plug in and out. It…ah…it's fucking *nice*. I wish you were here. I wish you were here so badly, doing all of this to me and being that horrible, crazy man."

"Believe me, so do I." I heard him swallow tightly. "But tell me more. I want to hear your voice. Talk dirty to me again, like we did in the hotel room, when I had you against the window. I loved the way you spoke, the words that fell from your mouth."

"Why, what was so special about it?"

"It was so honest. Raw and bare-boned. I need it again. I need that part of you again like I need my next breath."

His desperation, his need, seemed to reach through the

phone line and cocoon me. I wanted to give him relief and I wanted to give him that part of me. It sounded like he needed both pretty badly.

"Take your cock out of your pants. Grip it—hard—and hand-fuck yourself. Jerk fast, so your thumb rubs the ridge of the head, and when you move your hand back down, I want you to feel the softness of your bollocks on the side of your hand. Do it, Jacob. Do it now while I fuck both my holes. And speak to me like I'm just a body held captive for your perverse pleasure. Like I was in the alley."

"Ah, fuck! You filthy, dirty little bitch. If I had you again in that alley, I'd—"

"You'd what? Sink your dick inside me? Which hole? Which one do you really want?"

"I want both. I love your wet pussy, but I want to try your tight arsehole. Yeah, push inside until I can't push anymore, then pump until the pain goes away and you feel nothing but pure pleasure."

He wants the same as me, then.

"Are you fisting yourself?" I asked, by now jabbing the butt plug in and out, my other hand playing over my clit. That was dangerous territory, as my throbbing bud was just about ready to burst. "Is your cock getting harder the more you play with it?"

He didn't answer right away. The sound of his tattered breaths filtered into our room, and a crinkle, perhaps of the quilt or his shirt as he worked himself over.

"Yes," he managed, voice tight with lust and his concentration.

"Good. I'm going to come soon. Come good and hard. Imagine how I smell."

"I can smell you. Jesus, yes, I can smell you. Dirty bitch. Dirty...fucking...whore...of a...bitch."

His jagged speech turned me on more, and I rubbed my clit, circular movements interspersed with up and down. "God, I'm close. So fucking close." I thrust the butt plug harder, with faster strokes. "My arsehole's raw, so damn hot and raw."

"Your cunt. How's your cunt?"

"Wet. Dripping. I want you inside it. I...ah... God, I can't—"

"Come, bitch. Come for me. With me. Ah...uh-uh-uh..."

He'd reached the point of no return, a long, drawn out groan finishing his stuttered grunts. A garbled sound, one he made in his throat when he came, was drowned out by my sharp cry of pleasure as excitement spiralled in my clit and burst, spreading into my belly, my legs, and deep inside me. My arse clamped the plug hard, and I arched my back, abandoning the toy so I could pinch my nipples at the same time as I rubbed my clit faster, harder.

I hit the peak, thinking of Jacob doing the same, cum jetting out of him to land on his belly. The way he shunted his hips up with each expulsion, knuckles getting whiter, face screwed up with the intensity of his orgasm. I breathed out moans, my own orgasm fading, heart beating wildly and my legs trembling. My clit was too sensitive to touch now, and I moved my hand, caressing my stomach, then reaching down to take out the plug. It came free with a lube-wet plop, and I dropped it onto the bed and rolled onto my side, facing the phone.

Jacob's breaths joined mine, and for a moment we took the time to calm down from our highs. I wondered what he was thinking as my clit ached and my arsehole stung. Had he come so hard and fast because of lewd thoughts about ramming his cock into my arse?

I hoped so.

He spoke then, his voice thick, back to normal. "So, you have another fantasy?"

"I do. You want to join me in it?"

"Fuck, yes. But I don't want to hurt you."

"We'll be careful."

"Only if you're sure?"

His concern touched me. "Yes, I'm sure."

The sky had darkened further by the time we'd finished

talking and said goodnight. Stars glittered, easily seen without the hindrance of clouds. I couldn't see the moon, but the light from it brightened one corner of my view, the colour tinged silvery-blue.

I wondered if Jacob was still buzzing like me, and whether he stared out of the window at the same scene, wishing he was back here.

In bed. With me.

Tonight and tomorrow I would sleep alone, and then he would be home, as would the girls, our lives going back to normal until we made another reservation at a hotel or waited until the dead of night before we fucked. I smiled at the knowledge that our lovemaking had turned such a sharp, beautifully exciting corner, and the road ahead was littered with so many possibilities, so many avenues to explore.

I could hardly wait.

Suddenly, our sex life had got one hell of a lot more interesting.

Chapter Six

Two weeks later there was still no arse action and I was getting frustrated. Jacob and I had made love only once, missionary, in the still of the night, hoping the girls wouldn't hear us. One ear on the door and lips pressed tight to muffle moans, we'd barely moved, barely clicked into the lovers we wanted to be. The duvet had been pulled up over his shoulders despite our hot bodies, and I'd been hyper-conscious of the slight squeaks in the mattress.

It was just how it went sometimes. I'd had the time of the month, and Tess' asthma had played up, meaning she'd often come into our bed needing reassurance.

But thoughts of Jacob's cock in my arse wouldn't go away. If anything they'd intensified, become obsessive – almost. So on the second Friday since he'd come home from his business trip, I steadied my gaze on his over the breakfast cereal.

"Jacob, we need to get that spare room painted before your parents come to stay next month."

He didn't look up from scooping Weetos into his mouth and admiring a picture Lucy had done for her teacher's birthday.

"Sure, love, next rainy weekend we get."

"No." I dropped my voice to the authoritative tone I used when I really wanted to be listened to. "I think you should take Monday off. We could do it together."

"There's no rush, we have four weeks."

"Four weeks will fly by."

"Well, why don't you start and what you don't get finished I'll do in the evenings. You hate doing the ceiling, don't you?" He reached for his mug of tea.

"Jacob." I stood from the table and clattered two bowls together. "Take Monday off. We can do *it* then."

Lucy stopped chattering and looked up at me, eyes wide.

Jacob's gaze captured mine and he slowed his chewing. "It?"

"Yes, *it*." I pursed my lips, willing him to guess the hidden meaning behind my words. "It will take both of us. I really can't manage *this* on my own."

"Ah." His mouth curled into a sexy smile. "That. Yes, of course."

"You have three spare days of annual leave to take." I spun round to the dishwasher and began to load it. "See if you can book Monday off when you have that meeting with Dave today." I slotted in two crumb-coated plates.

"Shouldn't be a problem." He came up behind me and squeezed his groin into my arse, winding his fingers over my hipbones as I stooped. "Not much going on other than stock taking at the moment."

I stood sharply, instantly embarrassed by the hidden meaning behind the embrace.

"So sure, I'll book Monday off." He pressed his lips onto my ear and tightened his fingers further. "And I'll look forward to spending that time with you…decorating."

* * * *

The weekend went by painfully slowly, and I was in a permanent state of arousal. It seemed Jacob was too, and we had another silent bout of lovemaking on Saturday night.

"Love," he whispered, touching his damp brow to mine once he'd got his breath back from his orgasm. "On Monday, I…" His words ran dry.

Smoothing my hands down his hot back and feeling his cock soften inside me, I touched my nose to his. "What?"

"I'm not sure I want..."

Oh, shit, he was backing out. And I was ready, more than ready. I was desperate for it. "Want what?"

"To...you know."

I wriggled from under him, and he flopped next to me, scooping me against his body.

"Jacob? Tell me."

He sighed. "You know I loved our time in the alley."

"Mmm, yes, you've told me several times." My heart, having slowed slightly, now thumped away again, the threat of disappointment hanging heavy in my chest.

"Well, I know you like my forceful side when I'm talking to you or taking you hard, but—"

I gasped. "You mean you don't enjoy doing it? Oh, shit, now I feel stupid." Heat rose up my neck, prickling and sharp spikes of hotness.

"No, no." He cupped his palm over my cheek. "No, not that at all. It's fun. It's a new, exciting part of our sex life which I never thought we would experience. I love it, it's so hot talking on the phone and knowing I can be a caring husband and father or bad Jacob, the man who takes what he wants, when he wants."

My heart settled—a fraction. "So? What is it? What don't you want to do on Monday?" I blinked in the darkness and could just make out the whites of his eyes.

"I don't know if I can do the whole masterful thing while doing *that* to you for the first time." The words tumbled from his mouth as if he wasn't in control of them.

I remained silent.

"I know I talked about it in the alley when I was in character, but here, in our home, actually doing something I've never done before, to you or anyone, I want it to be us, real us. Not a game. This is special."

I reached out and touched his jawline, ran my fingertips over his stubble. "Of course," I whispered, relieved that he still wanted to fuck my arse but had just changed the way in which he wanted to do it. "I think that sounds a wonderful plan."

He blew out a minty breath that breezed over my cheek. "Thanks, love, 'cause I'm just so worried about hurting you and, well, your pussy is designed for me but that, *there*—it's not natural, is it?"

"It's natural to lots of people."

"But not us."

"Not yet, but I've been preparing."

"Preparing?"

I wasn't going to tell him, but it seemed it would help allay his fears, so I took a deep breath. "Yes, with the plug."

"You have again, even after that time on the phone?" His surprised voice was a little louder.

"Shh, yes."

"When?"

"During the day, when the girls are at school and you're at work. Twice I've used it."

"And masturbated?"

"No. I've just lain on the bed and pushed it in, slowly, getting used to it, the size of it."

"And have you?"

"Sort of."

"What do you mean?"

"Well, it's comfortable now, and it must be the width of two of your fingers at the base."

"That makes me feel a little better." There was a note of relief in his voice.

"Jacob, this is supposed to be fun, not something you should be worried about."

He tugged me tighter and twined his legs with mine. The dense hairs on his shins tickled. "I'm not really worried, love, especially after what you've just told me. I just want it to be special. It's kind of like taking your virginity again."

"Yeah, I suppose."

"I just know it's going to be amazing for me and I want it to be amazing for you, too, and I don't want anything getting in the way of feeling so close to you, so part of you."

Snuggling into his neck and tucking my hands beneath my chin, I sighed into my usual sleeping position. "It will be perfect, Jacob, I just know it will, and I trust you to stop if I can't handle it." As I said the words I knew he was trusting me too. I would have to make it right for both of us, the way he did for me so many times.

My arsehole had a lot to live up to.

* * * *

Monday dawned grey and drizzly. The usual scramble for school had me tense and rushing. Jacob stayed in bed, at my instruction, and I plonked a cup of sweet tea next to him as I raced into the room to grab a fleece and a book.

"I'll be back by ten-thirty. I need to call in at the chemist and the library. The books are due back today and the girls have so many out I daren't risk a fine."

Library fines bothered me, but I couldn't put my finger on exactly why.

"Sure." He grinned sleepily up at me. "You do that and I'll get ready."

I paused and twitched my brows. "Ready? I thought you were always ready?"

He smirked. "I am, but today requires extra preparation."

I brushed my lips over his. "Mmm, I like the sound of that."

The chemist had a long queue and I tapped my foot impatiently, willing the pharmacist to hurry. The library was quiet, but the absence of sound seemed to make the erotic images in my mind more vibrant. My anticipation more encompassing.

I was caught at every red light on the way home, and by the time I pulled into our drive my clit was buzzing, my heart racing and my arse cheeks had clenched so hard I was lifting from the driver's seat.

Bolting through the front door and throwing my keys and handbag down, I was suddenly hit by the sugary scent of vanilla. I paused.

"Jacob?"

"Up here, love."

I climbed the stairs, shrugging out of my fleece. His deep, steady voice was an aphrodisiac all of its own.

"In here."

The scent was stronger on the landing and the air held a hint of steam. I pushed into the bathroom, following his voice.

He'd drawn the blinds, and a long row of candles stood regimented on the windowsill, their flames shivering. The golden shimmer and heavy fragrances were startling after the dull Monday morning chores. It was like being transported to another world.

Jacob sat on the side of the bath wearing just black boxers, his skin shiny and his jawline unshaven.

"Hi," he said in a lazy, sexy drawl.

"What's all this?"

"I want you good and relaxed and I know how a hot bath with candles and a shoulder rub makes you all pliant."

"Pliant?" I grinned at the opportune use of one of my favourite words.

"Yes, pliant. Soft and mellow. Ready for me."

I stepped out of my shoes and tugged down my jeans and knickers. A hot bath with a shoulder rub sounded perfect. Because even I had to admit, my muscles and tendons were tight to the point of discomfort. Not good for what we had in mind this morning.

"Mmm," he said, eyeing my neatly trimmed strip of pubic hair. "You look good on a Monday."

I whipped off my sweater. "Don't I every day?"

"Yeah, love, I just don't often get to see you stripping naked on a Monday morning. It's a treat."

I flicked the clasp on my bra and cupped my breasts. Tweaked my nipples to hard little points as I jutted my hips jauntily.

He stood. "Get in the bath," he ordered, his voice rasping. "While I still have the self-control to give that shoulder rub."

Not wanting to miss out on the treat, I hopped in, faster than I should have. The temperature was lobsterpot hot, and I gasped as I sank low.

He shifted to the back of the bath, dipped his hands in the water, and set up a firm squeeze on the tendons between my shoulders and the nape of my neck.

"Mmm, that's nice," I said, the heat penetrating my skin as I breathed in the vanilla scent. It reminded me of my favourite cakes.

He dropped a kiss on the top of my head. "I want to make you feel more than nice, love. I want to make you feel like you're flying high."

I shifted on the base of the bath, and the piping hot water flowed into my pussy. Sighing, I shut my eyes. "Great plan," I whispered, thoroughly looking forward to the promise of flying high.

He continued to rub and squeeze, easing knots from my shoulders and scooping water and frothy bubbles onto my skin. The steam was heavy with our desire and the quiet splosh of the water echoed erotically around the tiled walls. I began to feel dreamy, his big, firm, familiar fingers transporting me to a wonderful place where only we existed.

Eventually he lifted his calming hands and I opened my eyes to the dim light.

"You ready?" he asked quietly.

The lust already pooling in my belly tugged at my pussy and clit, and my nipples peaked. I was more than ready. I'd been ready for weeks.

"Yes," I said, reaching for his offered hand.

He urged me up, helped me out, then wrapped a fluffy white towel around my shoulders. My skin was hot and tingly, the towel super-soft, as if my senses were heightened.

I leaned into him as he smoothed his hands over my back, drying and warming me further.

"That was perfect," I said.

Crooking his finger beneath my chin, he tilted my head. I stared into his face, his handsome, adorable face that I knew better than my own, and felt my heart would burst with love. What we were about to do I could only do, would *only* do, with him.

There was only Jacob.

Our lips connected and, in a sudden flourish, he scooped me up, holding me tight against his bare chest.

I linked my fingers behind his head as he kicked the door open and marched into our bedroom.

He searched my mouth with his tongue even as he lowered me onto the bed. I explored his mouth, too, absorbing his flavour, his texture, knowing I would never get enough.

As he dipped his head to my breasts, I noticed the candles set around our room. There was a hint of vanilla in the air here too, and briefly I wondered if he'd been out and bought candles especially. James Blunt played softly on the stereo Jacob had brought up from downstairs, his voice dreamy and calming.

"Mmm, you taste divine," Jacob whispered, nipping at my puckered areola.

I writhed for more. I wanted him to touch me all over. I was like a hot mass of wanton need infused with excitement.

"Jacob," I moaned. My patience had run dry. I needed him inside me, inside my forbidden entrance.

He must have sensed my urgency. "Turn over," he said and nudged me with flattened palms.

I willingly rolled onto my belly.

Scooping his forearm beneath my hips, he raised me and eased a pillow, and another, beneath my body.

"Just relax and let me do the work," he murmured, his breath warm in the hollow of my back.

"Yes, oh, yes, Jacob, please, now."

"Patience." He planted a hot, wet kiss on my left buttock

and wound his fingers up my thighs, easing them apart so he could sit between them. "Patience, my love. Let me adore you in a way I never have before."

I screwed my eyes shut and pressed my cheek onto the soft cotton duvet cover. This position was sexy as hell if he were about to fuck my pussy, but knowing his attention was going to be elsewhere gave it a whole new dimension. I squirmed and deepened the arch in my spine, offering my cleft up to his mouth as he kissed the globes of my arse.

My breathing quickened as he travelled the warm flat of his tongue down the crease between my arse cheeks. He kept going until he was actually licking over my puckered hole.

"Oh, God," I groaned into the mattress. Of all the things I'd imagined, having him put his mouth there was not one of them. My face burned. Even though I'd bathed… This was all so new, so… My whole life *that* hole had been mine, private, just known to me. And there was my husband, licking it. Could I cope with that?

The muscles in my legs tightened on his shoulders—my little warning that I was embarrassed—but he took no notice. Instead, he firmed his grip on my buttocks and stretched them apart, exposing my most secret place some more.

Letting out a groan of part mortification, part desperation, I twisted my neck to face the other way. The sight of the butt plug, my vibrator, and a tube of lube on the bedside table greeted me.

"Jacob," I gasped, needing to say his name as a whirlwind of thrilling images besieged me. Images of what was going to happen next. "Jacob."

He didn't reply. He circled and laved with his tongue, tapping over the taut wrinkles of puckered skin and smoothing over the flat flesh towards my pussy. Embarrassment left me and in its place the wetness of his mouth created a burning, furious whack of desire that seared right to the centre of my soul. This was as depraved as it was utterly glorious.

I was aware of his body heat on my back as he stretched upwards over me.

"You are simply beautiful," he said, reaching for the plug and lube. "Thank you for being mine." He sat back down between my legs.

Sinking my teeth into my lower lip because I couldn't answer, the lump of emotion in my throat too hard, I groaned and shut my eyes again. His hand was on my arse cheeks, and all I could think of was what was coming next. My clit swelled and buzzed and nothing had even stimulated it yet, my breasts were tight and heavy, pressed into the bed.

Then there it was—pressure at my hole. Cool, wide pressure—it wasn't the butt plug, it was the blunt tip of his finger.

"Let me in," he whispered. "Love, let me in."

I willed myself to relax as he entered me. It didn't hurt; I'd become accustomed to invasion now. It just made me impatient and eager for more.

"Oh, yes, Jacob, please, higher, touch me there. Touch me in there."

He didn't need asking twice. In a slippery slide he buried knuckle deep.

"Ah, yes," I said, fisting the sheets.

"Oh, fuck, you feel amazing."

"God, yes, so do you," I managed on a shaky breath.

"You're like satin, hot pillows of smooth, warm satin." He moved his finger, stroking my internal walls.

"More," I said. "Please, Jacob, I can take more."

He withdrew his finger, and I chased it with an upward flick of my hips.

"Easy, love." His voice was tight—he'd spoken in his calm voice, but I knew beneath the surface a vat of tension simmered. Sexual tension. I could just imagine how hard his cock must be.

Two lubed fingers were at my hole now, easing in. I

breathed deep, braving the sting in my circle of taut muscle and then welcoming the fullness he created when again he sank knuckle deep.

"Ah, fuck, yes that's it, your arsehole looks amazing," he said. "It's all stretched around my fingers."

Releasing my grip on the sheet, I sent a hand through a space between the pillows and sought out my clit. Began to circle to a slow, steady rhythm.

"That's it," he said, "you work yourself while I ease out this tightness."

Suddenly a slash of pain stung my rear hole.

"Ah, ow," I gasped.

"Shh, it's okay, I gotta get you open for me. My cock is wider than even the base of the plug."

I sped up my rotations on my swollen clit and visualised what I must look like from where he sat. Arse in the air, legs spread. My fingertips fretting fast over slick folds of flesh and my anus, my gaping anus, revealing itself to him as his fingers scissored in a series of ever-widening movements.

I closed in on myself. Only sensation existed. All my thoughts and emotions, every part of my physical being was zoned on what Jacob was creating in my body.

Suddenly, he withdrew his fingers and my arse clenched, the remaining sting erotic and dark.

"You want the plug?" he asked.

"No, no I just want you, Jacob, please."

"Are you sure?"

"Yes, I'm sure, please." I lowered and deepened my voice, surprising myself at how husky and dirty I sounded when I spoke. "Jacob, fuck me—fuck me up the arse, now."

The sound that erupted from his throat was more growl than speech, and in an instant the rigid crown of his cock was there; pressing, pushing.

The lube was cool, his cock hot, and when he pushed in that first inch, the sensation of the two temperatures mixing was a welcome distraction from the whip of pain snapping around my anal opening. It stung like a firecracker, burning and biting.

"Ah fuck, yes I'm in, love, you did it."

"Oh, God," I groaned. How would I be able to take any more of him? He was so wide and so unimaginably long to fit inside my small cavity. I continued to masturbate, harnessing and swapping the sensations spinning through my pelvis.

"I'm going in deeper," he said, wrapping his fingers around my hipbones and pinning me tight to the bed. "Tell me to stop if you need to."

I shook my head frantically. I wanted him to ride into me as much as I wanted him to get the hell out.

"Oh, sweet motherfucker," he moaned, as he slid further in.

"Oh God, Jacob," I said, the words thick and heavy in my throat.

He was so deep now, his balls nudged my engorged labia. The sensation was nothing like the butt plug. He was so wide; the whole length of him. Unlike the tapered shape of the plug, his cock was a dense rod of flesh, spearing me.

My muscles contracted, and I had an unbearable urge to expel him, to bear down. I opened my mouth in anguish, fearful of what was about to happen.

He withdrew. Not all the way, just so the head of his cock was inside me, the flare of his glans nestled against the inside wall of my arse. The feeling, thankfully, retreated.

"Karen, love, I'm not going to last long. This is fucking amazing."

I groaned in response. Worked at my clit and claimed the first spark that would lead me to orgasm.

"Are you okay?" he asked.

"Yes, yes," I panted. "But can I have the vibrator too? To send me over the edge with you." I stretched for it and he moved slightly with me so he didn't pop out. I tossed it downwards for him, and within a second its familiar humming filled the room. It was one of those vibrators with ears, tiny buzzing ears, and as he smoothed it into my channel, I guided the ears to either side of my clit.

Instantly, the sensations went up a level. I never stood a chance of lasting with the vibrator, and with him in my arse—well, I was already pulsing on the edge of orgasm.

"I'm going to fuck your arse harder now," Jacob said in a rasping voice that held more than a hint of the bad boy in him.

"Yes, yes, Jacob, fuck my arse, fuck me hard."

He drove in, his fingers tight on my hips and his cock claiming my body in a way it never had before. It was so utterly primitive and deliciously bad that I cried out—in discomfort, in ecstasy, at the wonderful fullness and connection deep within me.

He stilled. "Shit, I'm sorry, did I hurt you?"

"No, fuck no, Jacob, don't stop, please don't stop." I thrust backwards, trying to impale myself harder on him. The vibrator was so high, nudging my cervix, stimulating my G-spot. My clit was getting ready for take-off, and his cock, damn, his cock was burning and glorious, thick and wicked. An orgasm of the most intense variety loomed before me. But I wanted to prolong this moment before I grabbed it.

"Jesus, I can feel the vibrator," Jacob groaned, pulling back then steaming in again. "No fucking wonder it gets you off every time, it feels fucking fabulous."

I couldn't reply. My world had spiralled into a wonderful kaleidoscope of ecstasy. Carnal, primitive ecstasy. I was coming, it was there. Holding it off was impossible.

"Jacob, I'm, I'm…please, speak dirty to me while I… please…"

There was a pulse beat of hesitation then, "Ah, yes, I'm fucking your arse now, whore, really fucking your slutty fucking arse. Take it, take all of it, right up high."

As Jacob picked up to jackhammer pace, I erupted in a writhing heap of orgasmic wonder. Over and over, the waves crashed through me. I may have screamed in pleasure, or maybe the sound was in my head. I didn't know. I didn't care.

"You're taking it good up your arse, bitch. I'm gonna be doing this again real soon, whenever I fucking want to, ah, ha, fuck..."

A second orgasm ravaged my body, his words catapulting me onto a new high. My back and neck arched to breaking point, and my arsehole burned as Jacob plunged deep and spurted his cum into my passage.

"Oh, fuck, yes, yes..." he shouted, loud and uninhibited. "Fuck, that...is...it!"

"Oh, Jacob, Jacob. Oh, God, yes." My whole body pulsed; my arms and legs were spasming. His were too—I could feel his tremors juddering through him and into me.

Suddenly, his big body flopped over mine, his heaving chest hitting me square in the shoulders.

I grunted as air pushed from my lungs. "Jacob, the, the..."

"Jesus Christ, Karen, that's something else."

I wriggled and twisted. "The vibrator, turn it off," I gasped. The sensations in my pussy were overwhelming, the stimulation too much after two intense orgasms. My clit and G-spot were engorged and delicate—the toy still thumping into them was a wild discomfort.

Quickly he shifted, sought the base and withdrew it. He kept his cock lodged deep.

"You okay?" he panted by my ear.

"Yes, oh God, yes." I could hardly catch my breath. My heart raced and the sound of my heartbeat raged in my ears. "And thank you, thank you for the dirty words at the end."

He kissed my shoulder. "I'd do anything for you, you know that."

"Yes, yes, and I'd do anything for you."

We stayed like that for a long time, his cock in my arse and his chest hair scratching my shoulder blades. It felt right, perfect. Jacob and I had always been close but this was a whole new level.

I couldn't wait to do it all over again.

Chapter Seven

Being sore wasn't something I'd usually relish, but this time it served to remind me that another of my fantasies had been met. Every time I walked or moved, my arse ached, stung a little, bringing back memories of what we'd done the day before.

With Jacob at work and the girls in school, I wandered through the house, tidying absently with no real vigour for my tasks. My mind remained on yesterday, and I relived it time and again until I couldn't take it anymore. I risked having to rush upstairs and give myself some relief.

I'd turned into a woman who craved sex, just like the woman in *that* book.

But would Jacob be able to cope with my demands – ones I knew would grow with time? The days in between us being able to indulge freely were too many for my liking, and the planned weekend away couldn't come fast enough. Jacob's parents were coming to stay, to mind the girls while we went off on the ruse that we needed some special time over our anniversary weekend. Soon, the excuses for going away would dwindle.

What the hell would we do then?

I gripped the sink edge and stared out of the kitchen window into our back garden, at the large expanse of dark green lawn and the surrounding land – dips and swells of ground that went on for miles. We lived on the outskirts of town, our nearest neighbours far enough away that, if we had sex outside and I cried out, they wouldn't hear me. The thick stand of trees at the bottom, more of a copse, really, would be a perfect screen, shielding us from any prying eyes.

The next time they stayed over at Jacob's parents'...

I turned, walked through the house, the next chapter of that book playing on my mind—again. The place was so empty, so quiet. Maybe it was time I got myself back into the workplace. My brain was too idle, that was it. That was why I couldn't stop entertaining myself with sexual scenarios. But Jacob wanted me home, where the girls knew if they were sick I'd be here to care for them, not at work, trying to plead with a boss who had no intention of allowing me to go home. If I was honest, I wanted that too. Perhaps I could find something online that would allow me to stay home? I'd talk with Jacob about it, see what he thought.

Sighing, I had the abrupt urge to get out. To go somewhere, even if just for a walk.

I was lying to myself. I wanted to go and investigate the garden.

For places to have sex.

Instead of beating myself up over these new thoughts and desires, I shrugged away what was deemed 'right' and 'normal' and decided to fully embrace this new me. I'd said this before, but the old Karen kept creeping back in. Finding a balance between the two was proving harder than I thought. But I could do this, couldn't I? Other women managed just fine—and not just fictitious women.

Look, if I want to have sex outside again, why shouldn't I? The world won't go to Hell in a hand-basket if we fuck out there. Just because I'm a mother and a wife, it doesn't mean my life has to change to the degree that I lose my identity.

I'd already done that once and I wasn't about to do it again.

With fresh determination, I strode to the hallway, pulled on my boots and put on my coat, my mission firmly rooted inside me. With the keys and my mobile phone in my pocket, I left the house and walked around to the back. I stood in front of the kitchen window and glanced around.

A wooden table and chairs sat on the crazy-paved patio,

a brick barbecue beside them. I could lean over that table… A small fountain, water splashing over protruding rocks, gurgling in the quiet. Stretching out naked beside it on a blanket would be nice, but not until the summer. We could get one of those patio heaters, have a private barbecue, feed one another and drink wine until the cows came home. That would be a romantic night, nothing like the torrid, frantic fucks we'd engaged in so far. I found myself looking forward to it, filing that sultry summer evening into my mind for when the seasons changed.

I stared ahead at the trees, far enough away that we'd feel secluded, just us in the world with no one else in it. I smiled. *That* was what I wanted more than anything else. Yes, the sex was an added bonus, but it being just me and Jacob, concentrating on one another and not the girls, the bills, *life*…

Strutting across the damp lawn, I shoved my hands in my pockets. The day was crisp, with a bite to the air that chilled my fingers and pinched at my cheeks. A wayward breeze pushed my hair back from my face, and my eyes watered at the sudden assault. What would it feel like to have that breeze on my naked skin, the coldness perking my nipples? Springing goosebumps, Jacob's hands melting them away?

Exciting.

I reached the trees slightly out of breath, keen to find a suitable spot. Birds scattered at my approach, their safe haven invaded as I walked through the copse. Their squawks echoed, as did the sound of their flapping wings, and I supposed they were fleeing to roost somewhere else, waiting for the human to leave their place.

I gazed around, hands on hips, and frowned as I studied the area. The oak trunks were all rough, and I imagined the bark biting my arse as Jacob fucked me against one of them. My shoulder blades chafing. Twigs and natural outdoor debris digging into the soles of my feet.

It turned me on.

I ran a hand up the bark, skating over the knobbly

protrusions, skin tingling from the contact. Moss, soft as velvet in places, dusted my fingertips, and the image of my back and arse streaked with it after sex filled my mind. I almost asked myself what was wrong with me but stopped.

There's nothing wrong with me. I just...

I didn't allow the next thought to bloom. Constant analysing wouldn't change anything. I was different now, back to who I used to be, the young woman who had first met Jacob, and I just had to accept it. No more Mrs Good Girl, doing what other people thought I should. We'd do things our way, when we could, how we wanted. We'd plan it all out, right down to the last detail, and enjoy it.

There, I'd told myself off for the last time.

Feeling as though a burden had been lifted, I walked further into the mini forest, searching for a less ragged tree trunk. I found several, belonging to blackthorns. Two, with slim, relatively smooth trunks, stood close enough that if Jacob were to tie my wrists to each, I'd be spread-eagled between them, my body star-shaped and perfect for the germ of a new fantasy that popped into my head right then. I wasn't sure if I'd be able to lean over comfortably, though, without my shoulders and armpits screaming with pain. Would my tied wrists be able to take the strain? Would the ropes chafe my skin, leaving it sore and broken?

That wouldn't be so bad, would it?

I moved between the trees, reaching out to lay a hand on each trunk. Bent over to test the pain level. It wasn't much, and without the encumbrance of my coat and clothes I'd have more freedom. Jacob could stand behind me, too, with enough room to strike my arse using a twig with the bark stripped off.

Where the hell had *that* idea come from?

I knew really, just didn't want to admit it.

I stood upright, fingers tightening on the trees, my breath coming hard and fast. Exhilaration steamed through me, as though a part of my brain had registered that unlocking what I'd obviously held inside had produced a kind of liberty. And it had, hadn't it? As another gust of wind wended through the trees and ruffled my hair, flapping the open front of my coat so that they billowed at my sides, I had the urge to laugh. To let out all the old parts of me, the sound carried away by that wind, never to return. My smile hurt my face, but damn it felt good.

I dropped my arms to my sides and twirled in a circle, feeling young again, with a new purpose, new ways in mind to bring me and Jacob closer. Just us. Time together.

I wanted to strip naked, right here, right now, and dance around the garden, testing the cold on my skin, seeing if it fit.

I didn't.

Instead, I went back into the trees, my gaze on the ground in search of a sturdy yet flexible branch. One that wouldn't break when Jacob struck me with it, or hurt because it was too rigid. My few minutes' search proved fruitless—the branches were mere twigs—so I resorted to looking upwards and finding one I could snap off a tree. The perfect candidate jutted off a long, thicker branch, low enough for me to reach up and wrench free. It broke away, the jagged end sap-coated and smelling sickly. I ran my palm up and down its length then swiped it through the air in an arc to see whether the other, tapered end was *pliant*.

That word zipped a torrent of lust to my cunt, and I wished Jacob was home so he could bring me off, give me release. I brought my legs together, squeezed them tight to make the pulse in my clit go away. My stomach rolled with excitement as thoughts of what we could do out here swished through my mind. I imagined myself bound to those trees, a full moon hanging in an almost black sky, casting strong light that filtered through the leaves above and dappled the ground. From behind, Jacob's breath warmed my naked skin—my neck, one shoulder—his body heat so intense I knew he was almost touching me. I saw it as though I had already entertained this before, but I hadn't. It was all new to *me*, the wanting of this scenario, the tree branch, being tied to the trunks.

As with my other fantasies, once the seed of turning them into reality had been planted it grew, raging through me, growing tendrils that snaked off in different directions, different possibilities that could occur from one basic idea. For our first time out here—would Jacob even want to do this?—I wanted my original desire, but on other occasions… God, there was so much to explore. We could play out the rape fantasy again, Jacob chasing me across the garden as I escaped the house. He could be an intruder, intent on taking me in our bed, but I'd get away, come here, try to hide behind the thicker trunks. But he'd find me, take me roughly on the ground or bend me over that tree stump over there, the moonlight showcasing my bare arse and breasts.

Quickly, I walked towards the house and sat on a patio chair, beginning the task of stripping the bark from the branch. One scenario at a time, I told myself. We had plenty of days to investigate every single one that entered my mind in the future, and I hoped Jacob would provide some too. It would be interesting to know what he thought of in his private moments, what he wanted to do to me, and whether it was something I'd thought about too. Or perhaps there was something he wanted me to do to him.

I stripped the branch and felt along its new, pale skin, slapping it across my palm to test how it felt. A sharp yet pleasing sting. I had no idea whether it would turn brittle before Jacob used it. Did I need some kind of resin to stop that happening?

The sweet scents from exposing the layer beneath the bark wafted up, earthy and primitive, and gave me that sense of freedom that I'd experienced earlier. Was there something inside all of us, something archaic that harked back to the beginning of time, of man, where the aromas outside linked to our baser instincts? I had discovered something I hadn't thought would turn me on before, hadn't thought I needed—the burning desire to be taken in the open air with the smell of nature around me.

It was one of the most pleasant revelations I'd ever had.

* * * *

Jacob had called around one o'clock to let me know he'd be late home, something to do with him having to finish up some paperwork so it could be couriered tonight. At first I was disappointed. I couldn't wait to let him in on my new fantasy, but in a way it had been a Godsend. Trying to tell him while the girls were around—interrupting and just being within earshot, me trying to convey what I wanted in a coded way—wasn't ideal. No, I wanted to tell him every delicious detail, gaining his whole attention, with us relaxed in the knowledge that the children were asleep and wouldn't know what their parents were getting up to.

Seven o'clock rolled around, in the slow way hours do when you're excited about something, and I went about our usual nightly routine, bathing the girls and reading them a story. Once I'd closed their door and made my way downstairs, I had no idea what the books had been about. A touch of guilt got to me then—I'd been thinking of bundling the girls into bed and whilst doing it I hadn't given them my full attention.

In the kitchen, I lit the hob to reheat a beef casserole and put a pan of water on to boil for the potatoes I'd already peeled. With Jacob working late, I didn't want him coming home to a dried-out meal, or eating alone as he usually did. As the food cooked, I laid the table in the kitchen nook, placing a stout church candle in the centre and lighting it. We could chat about his day while we ate.

And then chat about mine.

Pleased I'd taken another step towards 'us time', I left the table and finished preparing dinner, my stomach contracting at the sound of his key in the lock. Was it silly that I felt like this, like a giddy schoolgirl who couldn't wait to divulge a secret? It was nice, this feeling, this new life we'd allowed ourselves. I waited with bated breath for him to go upstairs as he always did when he'd been working late, peep in on the girls, then return down here to me. In the past, he'd have found me sitting on the sofa watching TV alone, or reading, having already eaten. Things would be different from now on.

Only two minutes had gone by and he was already standing behind me, hands spanning my waist, his lips brushing up and down the side of my neck. I wanted to abandon dinner, turn to him and be held close, kiss him and forget the casserole and the table awaiting us in the corner. But a slow seduction called louder, eking the evening out so it would stretch on forever. Making me want him even more than I already did.

"Hey, you," he said against my ear. "Something smells good."

A shiver went through me. The good kind that tingled my skin and exited through the tips of my toes. "That'll be the beef." I stirred the casserole and switched off the heat, trying to act casual when all I wanted was to throw myself at him.

"That and you."

I smiled. God, I loved him.

"How come there's so much food?" he asked.

"I thought we could eat together when you work late. Take a breather just for us, instead of me in the living room, you out here. I don't want to lose what we've found again."

He squeezed me, brushed his cheek against my head, and a lump came unbidden to my throat. I thought of how, if we'd continued the way we'd been before, we could have lost so much. Maybe even found we had nothing in common anymore and taken the path to divorce. It had happened to so many of our friends. Damned if I'd let it happen to us.

He kissed the top of my head then moved away, leaning his elbow on the countertop as I walked to the sink and drained the potatoes. I blinked away the sting of tears and told myself we would be okay so long as we made time for one another. That was the key.

I *knew* he was watching me, watching my movements. His stare burned deep from behind, bringing back the memory of going outside and imagining him behind me in an entirely different way.

Fuck, could I get through this evening, holding back what I was bursting to tell him until after we'd eaten? As I dished up the food, I decided I could.

"Want some help?" he asked.

"You could pour some red wine." I smiled at him, loving the sight of every single angle of his face, his slightly stubbled jaw, the dark smudges under his tired eyes.

"Wine? Wow, we're going for it tonight." He reached into the drinks cupboard for a bottle, then went to get two glasses.

"Glasses are already out. I laid the table, look."

He glanced over to the nook, eyes widening a little. A slow grin spread, and he turned his head to look at me. "Do you have something in mind I'm not aware of?"

"I might have. You'll just have to wait and see."

A couple of minutes passed, Jacob pouring wine, me taking our meals to the table, and we sat, talking about his day, how Gerald, some new, irritating section manager, had riled him yet again.

He sighed. "Still, I'm home now. Work doesn't come into it." He chewed on some potato, swallowed, then took a sip of wine. "How was your day, love?" Before I could answer, he stared at a clear vase beside the candle. "And what the hell is *that* doing on the table?"

I fought the urge to laugh. At last, he'd spotted the branch. "Oh, that's a part of *my* day..."

Chapter Eight

It seemed Lady Luck had joined us for our journey, giving the green light for all our needs to be met only three days after my confession of what I really wanted him to do with that branch.

Jacob's parents had asked if they could take the girls to a circus on Saturday night. It started at eight, didn't finish until ten, so they'd suggested it was more sensible that they keep them until Sunday morning, possibly Sunday afternoon if the children fancied having a roast dinner with them at the local pub.

I was *not* about to turn that opportunity down, especially when Jacob had been hot for the idea of outside sex. In fact, he'd been more than up for it, and the excited glint in his eye when I'd held up the carefully stripped bark had sent a tremble to my very core. Something told me I'd hit another very dark and very sinful nerve of his.

But always one to think of others, Jacob had already promised to help a work colleague move house on the Saturday. I didn't mind too much because it left me with an empty afternoon to prepare for our evening of fun. I started with a pamper accompanied by a glass of wine, treating myself to a cucumber face mask, sugar body scrub, shave—including my pussy—manicure and pedicure and finally a generous slathering of body butter.

It left me feeling tingly and smooth, as if my body was honed and prepared. The thought of my silky, clean skin and perfectly neat red nails out in the open, amongst dirt and leaves, with the sootiness of bark mould smudged randomly over my body had me panting with excitement.

I could just imagine mud squelching around my toes and the creamy skin of my wrists worn red by ropes. And the image of my arse marked raw by the branch, well, that had me feeling like a sacrificial offering.

For I knew that this evening I would be handing myself over to nature, to Jacob, and to my own darkest desires. The bare bones of my soul were about to be revealed. No holds barred, no chance to hide. They were the very skeleton of me that only Jacob would ever set eyes on.

When the dipping sun sent lilac and crimson fingers darting over the horizon I was ready—more than ready. I'd had a light tea and another glass of wine, resisted the temptation to masturbate—just—and saved myself for my husband.

The front door opened with a whoosh, then shut with a resounding slam. I spun from the kitchen window where I'd been staring at the darkening copse.

The copse that was ready and waiting.

Heavy footsteps banged down the hall. Loud and resolute, the sound reverberated around my head.

This was it. There was no turning back.

I didn't want to. Not for anything.

The door swung open, and there he stood, with his broad shoulders filling the frame and his head bowed slightly. He pulled his brows low and set his jaw. A small muscle flexed and unflexed in his cheek.

"Get down on your knees, bitch."

I gasped at the completely thrilling sound of his bad man's voice and folded my legs until my knees landed on the freshly swept lino. He was so feral, so dominant, not Jacob the protector, the carer. No, tonight I had Jacob the master, the taker, the giver of sinful pleasure.

Between one breath and the next he was in front of me, his groin level with my face and his hands on his hips. The scent of man and hard physical work washed over me, as well as perhaps a hint of a greasy spoon cafe where he'd no doubt been treated to pie and chips for the efforts of his day.

"Take out my cock."

I reached for the buttons on his jeans, surprised to see that my hands trembled. Excitement? Trepidation?

This had not been part of any plan, but I wasn't complaining. In fact, there wasn't a plan. All Jacob had asked was that I trust him. He said that he understood what I wanted and would make it all happen for me. Of course, we had a safe word, but I couldn't imagine I would need it. I trusted Jacob with my life and my pleasure. I always would.

"Hurry up," he said, tangling his fingers in my neatly brushed, softly conditioned hair. "Take it out and suck it."

After I freed his cock, his length sprang into my palm, hot and thick, and the purple veins winding up the shaft bulged with his keen arousal.

In a sharp movement, he jerked forward and the tip slid into my salivating mouth. "Wider, whore," he snarled. "Take me, all of me."

I stretched my jaw and he sank deep, sliding to the back of my throat in one urgent movement. I gagged but he ignored it; pulled back then rode in again, all the time holding my head in a tight, vice-like grip so I had no choice but to take him, tip to base.

I'd sucked on Jacob's cock a million times, but never had he taken control like this. He was always respectful and deathly still, allowing me to determine depth and pace. But this was different—this was sinful, depraved Jacob fucking my mouth without a thought for my well-being.

I adored it.

Needing support as my body was jostled by his thrusting hips, I gripped his thighs. Saliva ran down my face and neck onto my red blouse, my nose repeatedly buried in his wiry pubic hair.

He steamed on and on, hissing and cursing above me. Breathing was difficult, my mouth was so chock-full of hard, demanding cock. When I did catch a breath the air was heated and smelt of him, musky and raw.

"Get fucking ready for it," he snarled, thrusting to such a depth his balls slapped against my chin. "I'm going to come down your throat. I'm going to fill you up, now...argh... fuck...now."

He let out a garrotted cry as his cock swelled further, then, in several sweet pulses, copious amounts of fluid gushed over my tongue. I swallowed rapidly, the action tugging the crown of his cock further down my throat.

"Ah, sweet...fucking...Jesus," he hissed, gripping my hair. "That's it, keep sucking, swallow me."

I did as he asked. My body quivered, and I could almost come myself just from the feel and taste of him climaxing so hard and forcefully. Had he lain there all those millions of times I'd sucked him off, restraining himself? Had he wanted to throw me down and fuck my mouth in a hard, abandoned way, but resisted?

I didn't have time to dwell on this because Jacob pulled out, gripped my upper arms and dragged me into a standing position. Gasping, I stared into his flushed face. His mouth was parted as he drew in big lungfuls of air. His eyes sparkled, the pupils wide and dilated, showing me the dark depths of his most basic needs.

"That's just the beginning," he said in a rasping, breathy voice. "To take the edge off what you've had me thinking of for three days." He slanted his mouth down hard over mine, taking possession of my lips and tongue in a furious, ravenous kiss. He pulled away abruptly. "You're such a tease," he muttered, "tempting me, turning me on. Well, now you're going to get it. You're going to get punished for making a man want you so bad it hurts his soul."

Fisting the lapels of my silky blouse, he stared down into my eyes. There was a sudden yank and my body jolted, air banged from my chest and buttons pinged onto the floor.

"You really don't need clothes," he said with a depraved grin. "Not for what's going to happen to you."

With another hard, ripping tug, my blouse was off and

thrown across the kitchen work surface. I hadn't bothered with a bra and my breasts hung heavy and aroused, dappled in shadows from the setting sun. I breathed quickly in short, snatching gasps, and my breasts were jostled with each intake of air.

"And these," he growled, snapping the button free on my trousers. "Get them off."

Hurriedly I complied, dropping them around my ankles so that cool kitchen air fanned over my bare pussy.

He tucked his softening cock away and twitched his brows as he registered my lack of pubic hair, but made no comment regarding the plump lips that peeked, softly rounded, from between my thighs.

"Outside," he said in a husky, dangerous voice as he glanced at the darkening window. "Get outside where I can give you what a slutty tease deserves."

He reached for my arm, and I stepped out of my trousers before he jerked me across the kitchen. His hold was rough and strong and sent a whole host of longing raging through my veins.

He flung open the door and marched out onto the bricked path that led to the patio area, then on towards the wilderness section of the garden.

The sensation of being naked, outdoors, for the first time was as exciting as it was illicit. It made me feel both vulnerable and empowered, a weird combination of emotions.

"Hurry," Jacob said, stepping off the path onto the grass.

The damp, dewy blades gripped my bare feet like fingers, and the feel of soft, cold mud beneath my soles was mushy and alien. I took a few jogging steps to keep up with him. My breasts jigged, as did my thighs.

The still air was a vast void of cool darkness that I'd suddenly become immersed in. My skin responded with goosebumps, as I'd known it would, but I didn't care, as I'd known I wouldn't. The heat raging in me was like a furnace. Bright and burning, enough to heat even the most freezing of nights.

We reached the copse. Jacob's big boots stomped over twigs, snapping them and shifting them out of his way. His breath was heavy; a slight fog misting from his mouth. Eventually, he stopped between the two trees that had been the centre of my sinful thoughts of late.

"You will only make a sound if I give you permission," he said, positioning me between the two slim trunks. "If you make any other noises you will be punished even more than you're already going to be."

I swallowed tightly and nodded.

He grunted before reaching for my left wrist.

Allowing myself to be handled like a puppet, I stood stock still on crisp leaves and dank earth as he wrapped a thick rope around my forearm. It was scratchy and hard, not at all pliable. He looped it over the first branch so that my arm was held up high. He repeated the action with my right wrist, silently, efficiently; so that both my upper limbs were out-stretched in a high crucifix position.

He stepped away and I heard the scrape of his lighter as he lit the four fat church candles I'd stood on squat bricks earlier. Instantly, a warm, golden glow bathed the cold woodland floor and flickered up the front of my harnessed, naked body.

"Mmm," he said, tugging his bottom lip with his teeth and studying me. "Perfect."

I swallowed tightly and breathed in the mulchy, earthy scent enveloping me. My clit swelled, trying to peek from its hood, and my nipples strained forward, the chilly air a caress to my feverish, needy body.

"Now I can do whatever I want and you can't do a thing about it." He lowered his voice to a sexy, dangerous drawl and tipped his face to mine. "Not a single…fucking… thing."

A shiver attacked my spine and jolted my stretched shoulder blades. He was so damn big standing before me in the shadows. Dressed in navy jeans and black sweater with his hair flopped messily forward, he looked menacing. Not the sort of man a woman would want to meet on a dark night.

He reached out and cupped my right breast, handling it not roughly but not quite gently either. He then watched his own movements carefully as he massaged and tweaked and tugged at my nipple.

Moisture grew in the deep well of my pussy. Hot and desperate need. I bowed towards him, wanting more than just my breasts to be fondled.

He stroked over my belly, dipping inquisitive fingers into the slit of my pussy. "Mmm, you're hot and ready for it, whore, aren't you?"

I pressed my lips in on themselves, remembering that I wasn't to make a sound.

He laughed, a deep, guttural noise that echoed around the tall, black tree trunks and drifted into the woody canopy above. "Good girl." He probed deeper and found my clit. "Keep nice and quiet."

I suppressed a gasp as he applied just the right amount of pressure in a sweet little circle over my clit. I was so turned on, so desperate for his touch. Perhaps he was going to treat me to a quick orgasm to get the night started on a high note like I had for him?

Parting my legs further, I shifted my feet on the squidgy, twig-strewn ground. I squeezed my eyes shut and embraced being naked in the woods—tied up and at one with nature, at one with Jacob and all the devilish, depraved things I would let him do to me.

His breaths grew ragged on my cheek, and his body heat radiated onto my trembling skin as he continued to build me towards climax. I opened my eyes and looked into his face. Shadows sliced over his angular profile, the candles providing the only light now in our small, dark woodland hideaway.

He kept up his heavenly rotations—he knew just how I liked it. My heart thumped, my breaths were getting harder to keep quiet and controlled. I was ready to come. Come while I was strung up outside, naked, between two trees.

He removed his fingers.

I opened my mouth to protest. *How could he? I was just about to climax.*

He widened his eyes, as if daring me to speak.

Hastily, I shut my mouth again.

"Ah, poor little slut," he said, cupping my chin with his damp fingertips. "Thought you were going to get some, didn't you? Well, now you know what it's like to be teased."

Despite the cold, heat rose on my cheeks—angry, frustrated heat. I yanked at the well-knotted ropes and they tightened on my wrists. If I hadn't been tied up I would have finished myself off. Two quick flicks was all it would take for a fast, sharp orgasm.

He stepped behind me and ran his flattened palm down the gutter of my spine. "So pretty," he murmured. "So pretty and perfect and just waiting for it."

As he slid his hand lower, I became aware that he was holding something else against my skin, something cool and plastic, pointed and moist.

"You have to take what I give you, whore, don't you? And right now I want you to take this."

It was the butt plug. Where the hell had he kept that hidden all day?

I rose onto my tiptoes as the narrow, lubed end traced down my cleft and poked at my puckered hole. Oh, God, I hadn't expected any anal play tonight. I thought we were doing something else. I wasn't psyched up for it, hadn't thought about it enough.

He nipped the ball of my shoulder with his teeth as the first section eased into my dark opening. I could say the safe word, but that would mean stopping our game, which, of course, I didn't want. So it seemed, again, I had no choice in the matter but to take it. Jacob could and would do to me whatever he wanted.

Willing myself to relax, because I'd taken the plug plenty

of times now, I breathed in the sharp, pungent air and concentrated on my tight ring as it expanded.

The plug eased in some more and I shuddered at the carnal bite of pain that besieged me. I was so turned on my entire pelvis was humming for more, but this caused the muscles to grasp the plug in an entirely different way to when I was lying on my bed, relaxed and alone, inserting it.

"I'm going to fill your arse then spank you," Jacob said into my ear, his hot breath instantly turning damp and cool. "Spank you, whip you, make you wish you weren't such a fucking prick tease."

I whimpered and hung my head low, the tendons in my neck stretched as my arsehole widened around the ever-increasing tapered length of the plug. He kept on pushing, on and on, paying no regard to my tightness until finally it popped into me, leaving just the wide arms poking at the underside of my buttocks.

"That's it," he said, almost soothingly. "That's you full."

Full!

Full was hardly the word. Stuffed, penetrated, out of control. They were the words that sprang to mind.

I'd become aware as I accommodated the plug that I was standing completely on my toes, like a ballerina. Glancing down through the flickering light, I saw my toenails had sunk into the ground. Dried leaves and jagged ends of twigs poked at the pale skin on the top of my feet and around my ankles. It was a sandpit of nature, the wood's own carpet, claiming me, becoming part of me. I was becoming part of it.

Arching my head up to the sky, I stared at the stark winter treetops. The moon had come out to play too. Its shimmering light fractured through branches as it stared down at our naughty game.

"Argh!" I couldn't help my shocked scream, and my whole body tensed. The wild, searing pain whipping over my buttocks was agony – tormented, frantic agony.

"Shh," Jacob whispered as he ran the barkless branch over

my tortured skin. "You'll earn more strikes if you cry out."

I sank my teeth into my bottom lip and willed my arse to release around its invasion. The involuntary clenching of my cheeks as he'd struck me had created a spasm around the plug, shoving it into the membrane separating my vagina and rectum. The sensation was both exquisite and tormenting. The more I clenched, the sweeter the internal pain.

"Brace," he muttered.

Brace! That was the problem.

Another stinging slap connected. Its thin, mean line created a cross-section of burnt flesh over both my buttocks.

"Oh, yes," he said, running his cool palm over my arse. "It's raised and swollen already."

I didn't doubt if for a second.

"It's a hot mark on cold flesh," he said. "A sweet line of possession."

No sooner had the pain retreated than another swinging slap rained down on my vulnerable skin. Owning me, blasting through me, releasing a huge shot of adrenaline into my system.

"Oh, God, Jacob," I murmured.

"I didn't say you could speak. Take it," he said hotly. "Take it where you need it most."

My befuddled brain tried to make sense of his words. Take it where I needed it most?

He struck again, the very top of my thighs this time. Oh my God! The flames of pain shot to my clit. Scorching the swollen flesh and making it bob within its hood. As I jerked away from the torture, I also found myself shunting back for more. The agony was like an electric circuit to my cunt, filling it with fizzing fire and wild, pulsing blood.

"Let it go," he said, thrashing my arse again and again.

"Ah, ah," I panted, absorbing the heat that bloomed across my skin and settled deep in my pelvis. The pain was like another living, breathing part of me, and I began to feel floaty as endorphins were released into my system. The world dropped away; I was drifting on a sea of sensation.

A sudden gust of breeze lifted my hair from my shoulders, and I flung my head back, relaxed my knees and allowed the ropes to hold my weight. The wind rustled around the branches and whipped over the leaf-littered floor. To my left the trees darkened, and I guessed one of the candles had blown out.

Jacob smoothed his hands over my arse, as if caressing the pains he'd inflicted. My clit was engorged. Moisture had seeped from my pussy and dampened the inside of my legs. I needed him to touch me again. I needed him to touch my clit and fuck my cunt.

"Soon," he said as if reading my hazy thoughts. "Soon."

The branch he wielded swung down again, the cold air shifting out of its way just a fraction of a second before it hit.

I moaned long and low, no longer mustering the energy to remain completely silent.

He picked up the pace, striking me fast and hard – they weren't pansy hits, they had real male muscle behind them and each lash bit like a snake. Before long they all blurred, each cruel sting meshing with the last until my arse was just one thrumming mass of pain.

A barrage of emotions overwhelmed me as I hung there, in the dark woods, my arse penetrated and being beaten by Jacob's branch. I never would have thought I'd have this experience, but it was so liberating. Jacob inflicting this erotic pain had given me a whole new level of sensation. A whole new understanding of myself.

As suddenly as it started, the beating stopped.

I didn't move, just allowed myself to be suspended by the ropes as I panted through the pain and listened to my pulse raging in my ears. My buttocks and the tops of my thighs were on fire, burning, and as the cold night stroked over them they sizzled and stung.

"Look at me."

Jacob pinched my jaw between his fingers, and I opened

my eyes. He was naked now, and the shadows from the candles flickered across his wide, defined chest. He reminded me in that instant of a Roman soldier, bronzed and sculpted. A thin layer of sweat shone in the hollow of his throat and over his top lip, and his fringe was jagged over his forehead.

I loved him like I knew I would never love anyone else.

He stooped and slotted his strong, corded forearms under my thighs, hoisting me into the air so that my spread pussy was directly over his cock. "You can speak now. Tell me what you want, bitch."

"I-I want you to, oh, please, please just fuck me." Winding my fingers around the ropes I could reach with my new elevated position, I jerked and tried to impale myself on him.

He grunted and allowed the first inch of his cock to push in. But he had me in a tight hold and I couldn't drop down any further than he would allow.

"You gonna tease me again?" he asked harshly.

"Jacob, I... I...please, yes, yes. Whatever you want." My pussy was contracting around nothing–I needed filling, now.

"Because whenever you want tying up and punishing, all you've got to do is tease me and you'll get it." He pressed his mouth to mine in a heated kiss. "And, just so you know, whenever I want to put that plug in your tight little arse and fuck your pussy, I will. You're mine; I will do to you whatever the hell I want, whenever I want."

His words were like an aphrodisiac and my arse clenched around the plug, stimulating me so much that an orgasm hovered. If only he would...

He thrust in, right to the hilt.

I cried out. My channel was so tight. With the plug in place his cock felt so much thicker, so much wider. The stab of pain was deliciously bad, and the sensation of being invaded and filled overwhelmed me so much that tears fell.

"Shh," he soothed against my cheek. "Shh."

But I didn't want to be quiet or soothed. I felt wonderful, and no one would hear us. I wanted to shout and scream and let Jacob know how fantastic he made me feel. They were tears of joy. "Jacob, Jacob, please, oh God, yes, yes!" I shouted. My orgasm was so close. One more stroke.

He pulled me off his cock, then, using the ropes I was harnessed to, swung me back down on to him.

For an aching, eternal second I stiffened, my body waiting, suspended, knowing it was there, finally. "I'm coming, I'm coming, I'm coming," I panted, staring down at where we were joined. His dark pubic hair was mashed against my clit; his hips had reared upwards as he thrust as deep as possible into me.

"Fuck it, yes, yes," he hissed.

He shoved me up and banged me down onto him again, the penetration bordering on violent.

"Argh!" I erupted in a rolling, hanging mass of ecstasy. My anus clenched around the plug and my pussy squeezed and milked his cock. My clit sent shockwaves of wanton bliss careering through me.

"Oh, fuck, that's it," he cried out, his voice now every bit as loud as mine and his head thrown back. "That is fucking it!" He came deep inside me, ramming my body down onto his over and over.

I split apart again, my body reeling in a million different directions in the cold, dark woods. It travelled from the tips of my fingers, frantic and bloodless, right to the ends of my filthy toes.

What on earth had we become?

Chapter Nine

I'd decided to try and persuade Jacob to confess his deepest desires. It struck me that it hardly seemed fair, him accommodating every one of my fantasies so far and me not doing the same for him. Our relationship had always been based on sharing, and, although I was delirious with happiness that he was willing to cater to my needs, it didn't feel right. Off balance, somehow. The challenge was whether he would express aloud what he'd previously kept in his head. Granted, my opening up had shown me a side to him I never knew had existed, and his reaction, the way he played the part so well, that dominant, brute of a male, told me I'd tapped into one of his desires already. And then there was the blowjob, him holding my head, choosing the pace and directing exactly how he wanted it to be. I had no idea he'd wanted to act like that. I'd supposed he was just a gentleman, wanting it sweet and sexy as opposed to rough and ready.

Again, I wondered – were there more sexual secrets he'd kept hidden, lingering under the surface, him waiting for the right moment to let them out? Was he like I'd been, wishing he could blurt it out but fearful of my reaction?

I thought about how well things had gone recently, how each new sexual scenario had worked as though we'd acted them out before, even though it was only me that had read about someone else enjoying them.

But we'd always known what the other had wanted and needed on this journey so surely that should tell him it was okay to push for more. Did he need courage? A little prodding?

I aimed to find out. Imagine if his needs matched mine or sparked ones I had no idea I'd wanted until he'd spoken…

I recalled how I'd felt in that hotel room when I'd told him about the rape fantasy. It had been embarrassing, awkward even, to utter the first words. But once I knew he understood, didn't think me dirty, I relaxed. Perhaps he needed the same from me.

I'd coax the words out of him if it was the last thing I did.

The opportunity presented itself, once again convincing me fate was on our side. Jacob was working late. I'd cooked a delicious meal, set the table, and planned on bringing his fantasies out into the open.

I imagined his voice, hesitating at first to tell me what he wanted, and I swear my heart swelled with love for him as I placed the girls' school uniforms in the washer and switched it on. He was such a beautiful person, and I knew him becoming that rough, domineering man in the bedroom must have been like wearing clothes he'd never have chosen without someone telling him they suited him.

But, my God, he'd settled into that role so well, so easily. I could only imagine what the future held. So many fantasies to play out, so many to combine to make new ones. The possibilities were endless.

With the washing machine humming and sloshing, our dinner—chicken chasseur—cooking in the oven, and the girls already in bed, I made my way upstairs for a quick shower. Taking my clothes off sent a frisson of excitement through me. I'd become more comfortable with myself naked lately, despite the jiggling thighs and wobbly belly. Jacob didn't seem to notice. His adoration of my shape, the way he brushed his fingertips over my skin, following the contours—the incline, apex, and downward slant of my hipbone; the curving dip of my waist; the rounded swell of my breasts—told me all I needed to know. He loved me as I was. The new clothes I'd bought while we'd been away had helped too. I still wore my favourite jeans and tops, but every couple of days I put on a dress or a skirt with a blouse instead. Jacob's reaction when he came home and saw me wearing them made me want to buy a whole new wardrobe.

Maybe I would next week.

I shaved my pussy again, reminding myself to find the courage to have it professionally waxed. If he liked it this way, I'd keep doing it. I admitted I liked the idea of never having hair there again. Besides, it felt good against my fingers when I fondled myself. When I was alone, masturbating, I tilted my hips so I could look down at myself and see my fleshy wet lips, fingers gliding between them. The sight always made me come quickly.

Dried and dressed in a calf-length black négligée, I went back downstairs to await my man, idling away the final minutes by tweaking the white roses in the vase on the table, straightening the polished cutlery, opening the oven to check the food. Repeating those actions until I was sick of them.

The wait was killing me.

At lunch, Jacob had telephoned to say he'd be late—he always did if his arrival home would be after seven—and the routine of that had made me smile. We had a pattern, things we always did, ways we always followed, and they brought security. Too much security. I knew that now, because we'd almost let it overwhelm us, take us where it wanted. We'd allowed life to direct which road we took instead of us choosing. Now, although the same routines were in place, new ones had arrived, yet they hadn't upset the balance. If anything, they'd enhanced it.

I was so thankful for that. We still *had it,* still wanted each other as much as we had when we'd first met. More, even. And wasn't that saying something? The first flush of love had been a heady rush of emotions, all-consuming, threatening to cut off my breath, and every thought in my head was about him. I could think of nothing else, and now it was the same way. I liked to think we'd fallen in love again, rediscovered why we'd become a couple in the first place, and God, it felt so damn good.

His key scraped into the lock, and my stomach rolled over then clenched so tight I thought I might be sick. It felt like I hadn't seen him in forever, had waited years to be with him again. Excitement bubbled inside me, my knees weakening at the sound of his tread on the stairs, the faint squeak of the girls' bedroom door opening, the soft thud as he closed it after checking on them. He'd be down here soon, standing in the kitchen doorway, filling the frame as well as he filled my cunt—to capacity.

Absurdly, I had the urge to position myself, a seductive pose that would have him thinking of nothing but me. The hunger in his belly would vanish, replaced by an entirely different kind that tightened his balls and lengthened his cock. I felt like a schoolgirl again, giddy with anticipation, and darted about the kitchen trying to find somewhere to drape myself before he appeared. Why was I doing this? Why, all of a sudden, was it so important that I be different? Was taking the dinner out of the oven not an act I wanted him to see anymore?

I admitted that it wasn't, not on these nights anyway. They were for us, domesticity thrown out the goddamned window. I wanted to be the woman of his dreams, sexy and someone he couldn't wait to run his hands over. He'd say I already was, but I wanted to *feel* it.

I spotted a rose petal on the rug beneath the table, a stray lemon-shaped splash of whiteness against the red pile. I wanted this to be perfect, *right,* and went down on hands and knees to pick it up before he came in.

"Well, hello, love!"

His voice sent shivers down my spine, knotted my tummy again, and brought a blush to my cheeks. He'd caught me being domestic, and I hadn't wanted that.

"Are you waiting down there for me?" he asked.

That sentence, it had a touch of laughter in it, yet at the same time was husky and all kinds of wonderful. The burn of anger at being caught like this melted away. I turned to look at him, not in the doorway as I'd imagined but by my side, propping himself up with one broad hand grasping a dining chair.

The sight of him, all wide shoulders and tapered waist, his suit crumpled from sitting at his desk and the drive home, brought on a spear of love so violent I wanted to cry. This man was mine, all mine, and I was one lucky woman.

I clutched the rose petal in my fist, likening its silky feel to that of his hard cock, and feigned nonchalance, as though he caught me on my hands and knees every day of the week. "Oh, I just spotted something under the table." I stood, conscious of my négligée swaying, the fabric brushing my legs. "Hungry?"

The gleam in his eye expressed his desire and my nerves settled a little. It would play out just as I'd hoped, wouldn't it? I cursed myself for this sudden uncertainty—did I want everything to be so perfect that badly? Yes, I did. I needed the mood to be right so Jacob would confess without feeling exposed. Baring his soul would take a lot—he wasn't used to it.

"I see we're sticking to our evenings alone when I work late, then."

He stared at me, seeming to see right into my soul, as though he knew exactly what I'd planned to discuss. Was I that transparent? Did he know me *that* well? I supposed he might, us having been together for so long, and if that look was anything to go by, he was more than willing to play the game.

I'd underestimated him.

I stood there, staring back at him, the gap between us too wide even though it was merely inches. I wanted to breach it, close it so nothing was between us except our clothes, but something was happening to prevent it. One of *those* looks, where speech isn't necessary, where touching isn't important. A meeting of two souls in complete understanding of one another. It touched me so deeply I snatched a breath and heard the soft hitch of a sob brewing.

Relief poured into me, because damn, I'd begun to think it was all about sex, that we had become crazed, only wanting one another for pleasure. That wasn't the case, I saw that now, and I couldn't help myself. I darted forward, pressed myself against him, never wanting to let him go.

"Hey, what's the matter?" He circled his arms about me, crushing me to him, and kissed the top of my head. "Did something happen?"

"No. Yes. But nothing bad. I just love you, that's all. I just wanted..."

The rest of my sentence failed to emerge. I didn't need to say anything more, really. He knew.

Jacob stroked my back, the heat from his hands drawing out every bit of anxiety. He always did that, had the ability to make even the worst days seem better. I belonged with him, couldn't imagine being with anyone else.

"You look lovely. Smell lovely," he said, lifting one hand from my back to slip his fingers beneath my chin and tilt my head up. He looked into my eyes, stared for long moments. "I love you."

He said it so easily, so simply, the words full of much more than what he had actually said. He cradled my head, thumb gently brushing my cheek, and a soft smile stretched his lips. I knew what he was thinking—I was thinking the same things myself. That we were lucky to have one another; that our love was real, and I thanked God for the day he'd sent Jacob to me.

He broke the spell. "So, other than eating, did you have anything else in mind?"

"I did, but if you're thinking of sex, if we indulge now it won't be one of our mad efforts."

"No." He paused to look at me some more, gaze probing, loving. "It wouldn't."

It would be a gentle exploration, all slow touches and long, soul-searching kisses. But we had yet to discuss his fantasies, and if they were hot, who knew how the sex would be then?

Who was I kidding? It would be searing, rampant. Filthy.

I broke away before we gave in to temptation. If we did, I imagined we'd eat in the living room afterwards, ignoring the beautiful table, snuggling beside one another in that sated way we had when sex became lovemaking. I'd possibly coax words out of him, but there was the chance he'd laugh them off, diverting my attention with kisses and strokes, him letting me know he was ready for round two.

No, I had to find out what he wanted.

I walked to stand in front of the oven, smiling at the fact that the oven gloves I slid over my hands were hardly what anyone would call sexy. I must appear incongruous to him, a woman in a cock-hardening negligee, the image spoilt by huge, quilted red mittens. I went through the motions of serving dinner. Heard him pull out a chair, the scrape of the feet dulled by the rug. Knew he was sitting from the creak of wood and shuffle of clothing, and watching me.

"That nightie is see-through."

"I know."

"Is that why you put it on?"

"Might have been." I smiled, adding roasted potatoes to our plates.

"I can see your arse. Your whole body."

"I imagine you can." Here was my opportunity. "What does it make you want to do?"

A few beats of silence followed that question. Had I blown it?

"Makes me want to watch you when you wear it."

"Does it make you want to touch?" I carried the plates to the table and placed them on the mats as though what we were discussing was an average couple's dinnertime conversation.

"Yes, but no."

I tried to hide a frown, I really did, but it came all the same. "Oh?" I sat, not opposite, that was too far away, but on the other side of the table corner from him. It would be easy for me to reach across and hold his hand that way if he needed assurance, or rub my foot over his.

He picked up his knife and fork. "I like the way..." He sighed. "I like the way your body moves under it. And I want to umm, want to see...want to not be able to, uh... You know what I'm trying to say, don't you?"

"Sort of." I knew exactly what he meant, but wanted him to *tell* me. I cut into my chicken, popped a piece into my mouth, busied myself with eating so he wouldn't think I was hanging on his next words. I longed to look at him, but if he was about to go into detail, giving him my full attention wasn't going to work.

"Like...like a 'look but don't touch' thing."

I lifted my eyes a bit, watched him cut a potato in half. Steam rose from the creamy flesh inside the crispy outer casing. He moved on to cut his chicken, pushed a few mushrooms around. He was nervous and I wanted to make it all go away, but if I could reveal my secrets, he'd have to learn to reveal his. I felt cruel, remaining quiet.

"*Can't* touch," he said quickly.

Heat pooled between my legs. Was he suggesting what I thought he was?

I swallowed my food. "Oh, right." It came out blasé, as though he wasn't trying to tell me something he'd never spoken about before. Like it didn't matter. That was an understatement. It mattered—more than he realised. It was important to me that we were back to the sharing thing, taking it in turns. If I pushed it, asked questions that sounded too direct, he'd back off.

He released a long breath. "You ever...you ever wanted..."

I felt for him, struggling like this, and it took every bit of willpower I possessed not to say it for him. I speared a mushroom, ate it. Speared another as he toyed with his food. Poured wine, red and rich. Pushed the stopper back into the top and swirled it around my glass, pretending to be fascinated by the burgundy stain it left just below the rim.

"D'you like being tied up?"

There, he'd said it. Got it out. And I knew I had to act fast before he burnt up with shame. I looked up, spotted his rigidity, how uncomfortable he was.

I grinned. "Damn right I do. Think you'd like it?"

Relief bled from him, shoulders relaxing, his blush searing hotter in spite of his obvious discharge of tension. "I've wondered what it'd be like."

Finally, he ate some food.

"I did too. The not being in control. Not being able to touch. It sounded exciting – and it is." I sipped some wine, eyeing him over the rim of the glass.

He nodded. "Never thought you'd want to try that, though. On me, I mean." He rushed on. "Knew *you'd* like being tied, but..."

If that food danced about beneath his fork any longer...

"You want to try it? See if you like it?" I laughed, easing the tangible strain in the air. "We've tried my ideas, why not yours?"

"It doesn't sound...unmanly to you?" Another potato cut in half. More steam.

"God, no. Sounds sexy as fuck."

He smiled then, the use of a dirty word clearly making him feel better. "What, you into being dominant too?"

"I could try. We might see another side of me."

"I like these sides." He looked at me, lopsided grin reaching his eyes.

"Me too. So, you want to try this when we go away?"

"We could do." He shrugged.

Now who was feigning nonchalance!

"We could do? Is that it? All you can say?" I laughed lightly. "I may as well get into my role now, try it on for size. *Could do.*" I smiled, a sexy one that didn't need any practice. "We *will* do."

Chapter Ten

I splashed out on our anniversary weekend away. It hadn't been intentional, but when collecting Tess' prescription in town, I saw an advert for a package trip to Amsterdam in the window of the travel agents. Half price from our local airport, room upgrade, transfers and breakfasts thrown in. It hadn't taken me more than thirty seconds to make my decision.

Amsterdam was somewhere I'd always wanted to go. The lure of the art museums and the romance of walking along the canals was strong, but now there was also the thought of venturing into the red light district, seeing whores sitting in windows offering their services to punters. Or, and this was something I really fancied, perusing sex shops without worrying that I would bump into someone I knew – something that had kept me from the blacked-out-windowed shop on the edge of town.

My curiosity had become burning of late as to what was held on the sex shop shelves. Jacob's confession that he wanted me to dominate him, tie him up and do whatever I chose to his big, gorgeous body was becoming more appealing by the hour. My mind was full of new thoughts, new decisions. What should I wear? Should I stock up on extra secure handcuffs? My man was strong, and if teased, heaven only knew what he would be able to break out of. Should I slip into role before tying him up? Make him crawl around our hotel room and kiss my toes, lick the arches of my feet?

It had all been hypothetical, but now, on the morning of our first full day in Amsterdam, I was ready to put my plans into action.

The Rijksmuseum was stunning. The Rembrandts everything I'd hoped they would be. Jacob held my hand and patiently waited at my side as I read the details of each masterpiece. But although I looked calm and studious on the outside, inside my stomach was tight and my heart fluttered.

When we'd arrived, tired and hungry late last night, I'd spotted a shop down a backstreet near to our hotel. The garish purple lights around the window and the flashing sign above the door—*Male and Female Play*—had me angling to go and check it out. Okay, so it wasn't cultural or educational, but for me, and what I had planned for Jacob, it would, I hoped, be perfect.

Eventually, after a delicious lunch in a small cafe, me salad, Jacob burger, I declared that I was tired and could we head back to the hotel for an afternoon nap?

"Sure, love." He gestured to the bottle of beer he'd washed his burger down with. "I'm not used to having a drink at lunchtime. We could go and lie down."

His cheeky smile reassured me he wasn't all that sleepy. Perhaps he had the same thing in mind as me—making the most of once again having kid-free hours and a nice hotel room. Only this time it was Jacob's turn. I was going to fulfil his fantasy the way he'd so expertly and graciously delivered mine.

Linking arms, we stepped out into the cool but sunny day. Jacob chatted about work for a few minutes, then I switched the subject to our surroundings. The glistening canal, the medley of house boats complete with potted plant gardens, the locals whizzing past on their bikes and the grand houses standing tall and proud around us.

As we neared the hotel, I started to panic that we'd gone past the sex shop. I glanced down several alley-sized passageways, desperately searching for the sign again.

Finally, I found it.

"Jacob," I said, halting. "Shall we just have a look down

here?"

He frowned and peered into the shadows of the narrow, cobbled street. "Why? Doesn't look like there's much down there."

"Please, just for a minute."

He shrugged, and when I tugged his hand he stepped in line with me.

As we drew level with the shop I glanced at his face.

He raised his brows and turned to me. "You are a very naughty girl when let loose," he said with a wry grin.

"I know, and it's you who's let me loose."

He gave a deep, rumbling chuckle.

"It looks open," I said, indicating the lights around the window, which, although not as bright as last night, were definitely on. "Can you wait here a minute. I need to get some stuff. Alone."

"Well, I'm not sure that's a good idea." He frowned. "We don't know who's in there or what it's like."

"It'll be fine and I really need to do a bit of shopping for… you know."

He shifted from foot to foot, his shoulders tensed.

"Jacob…" I brushed my lips over his. "Wait here, five minutes, ten max, and then I promise you," I lowered my voice and pressed my body to his, "I'll be all set to give you the time of your life."

He hardened his jaw and his eyes flashed. "Five minutes. Be quick and don't spend too much."

I grinned. "I will, I won't." Quickly I stepped away and, before he could change his mind, pushed into the shop.

The bell above the door announced my arrival and the warm, oil-infused heat surrounded me. I was shopping.

My sort of shopping.

* * * *

Okay, so I blew my entire budget. Who knew this stuff would be so expensive? I'd been secreting away housekeeping for several weeks *and* had dug into my emergency jar, but it still didn't buy everything I wanted. Enough, but not everything I'd had in mind.

But now, standing in the hotel en suite, I skimmed my hands down the smooth PVC corset I'd bought and felt satisfied with my purchases. The corset had a thick silver zip at the front and the tight bones nipped and trimmed my waist dramatically. It was unusual in that it had a halter-neck attached and the thin material over my breasts was black fishnet. It felt lovely over my areolae, ever so slightly scratchy, as if the very point of my nipple might poke through. My breasts were certainly visible, heavy and creamy beneath the black criss-cross.

I'd found long fingerless gloves in the same fishnet material in a bargain bin along with black, silky crotchless panties with tiny zip details over the hips. I didn't really have the sort of arse for such high-legged, skimpy sexiness, but I didn't think that would bother Jacob. He'd seemed particularly keen on my arse these last few months, giving it extra attention whether I was standing at the sink or if he was making love to me. Yes, the panties would work, especially since I'd pulled them on over fishnet tights, also crotchless – I had themes going on; crotchless, fishnet.

My legs looked longer than they ever had before, not least because of my most expensive purchase. My most lavish extravagance – knee-length boots with spiked silver heels. They were without a doubt the most erotic footwear I'd ever bought. I'd loved them instantly, and straight away an image of Jacob lying on the floor, me standing next to him in those boots, trailing a whip over his chest had flown into my mind.

I had to have them.

I pulled in a deep breath, leaned towards the mirror and finalised my look with 'Vamp Red' lippy and a squirt of heavily spiced 'Decadent'.

Jacob was in the bedroom, waiting for me. I hadn't shown him any of my purchases when we'd arrived back at the hotel room, simply told him to shut the curtains, strip off all his clothes and wait for me.

It had felt good, trying out my dominant side, even if I'd added 'please' at the end of the sentence.

But not anymore.

When I stepped out now as Mistress Karen, I would not be asking, I would be telling. If I desired Jacob to do something, I would expect to be obeyed.

I reached for the bag of purchases that weren't for me. They were all for his entertainment.

Pulling open the door, I was pleased to see Jacob had drawn the curtains on the two narrow windows that overlooked the Skinny Bridge. The muted glow in the room was provided by one bedside lamp and shards of daylight from the outer edges of the curtains.

Jacob sat naked in the chair, his hands curled over the arms. He widened his eyes and swept his tongue over his bottom lip as his gaze trawled my sexy new outfit.

I strolled towards him, rolling my hips with each step and delighting at the way my spiked heels sank into the plush carpet. Cool air washed over my pussy and my labia felt engorged with arousal even before we'd begun. I'd never felt so feminine, so in control, and despite the nerves in my belly, a surge of confidence rippled through me. I knew what I wanted to do, and I knew that Jacob wanted it too. There was no need to be nervous.

"On your knees," I ordered, dumping the bag on the table, covering a magazine about Amsterdam's entertainment and the room service menu.

He slid to the floor, folding his legs beneath him. His engorged cock was heavy and bobbed as he moved. As he sank, his broad shoulders were suddenly highlighted by a slim streak of light coming through a gap in the curtains. I thought about drawing them tighter, but the sight of the dust motes dancing around his flesh was almost ethereal and I couldn't bring myself to change the moment.

"Today I am in charge of your pleasure," I said, delving

into the bag. "Which means there are three rules. You will do as I say. You only look directly at me when I allow you to, and, most importantly, you will only come when I give you permission. Do you understand?"

I pulled a black and red flogger from the bag. The leather handle was smooth and had a domed end that reminded me of the head of a cock. The fifty tails were made of thin suede and swished softly as it moved. Like the boots, the flogger had called to me from amidst a huge selection of paddles, bullwhips and crops. I reckoned it would suit my needs. Jacob hadn't asked for erotic pain the way I had with the branch, but I thought its tickling ends would be a great way to tease and titillate my captive. Make him a little unsure of my moves and increase the anticipation.

"Karen – ?"

"Did I say you could speak?"

I used a harsh tone and flicked the tails of my flogger at the ball of his shoulder. They flew through the air and connected a little harder than I'd intended, giving a sharp slap as they struck.

But he didn't wince or jerk even a fraction, just swallowed tightly and gave a stiff shake of his head. His cock twitched.

Ah, so he liked the flogger inflicting a little pain.

As I stepped around him in a complete circle, I ran the tails over his chest, upper right arm, and back, swaying my hips and exaggerating every movement of my legs and arms.

I paused by his face to make sure he was under no mistake that my outfit was crotchless. "The flogger is for when you are tied up and can do nothing about where and how hard I decide to touch you."

After resting it on the chair he'd been sitting on, I went back to the bag. This time I pulled out two pairs of silver handcuffs. I'd had a dilemma when we'd arrived and found the headboard to be a neat, shiny affair attached to the wall. There were no sexy wrought iron bars or strong wooden posts to secure Jacob to. But my problem had been solved with the mental image of him on the floor and me in my boots strutting around him. The solution was exactly that, the floor.

"Do you like my outfit?" I asked.

Silence.

"You may speak."

"Fuck yes."

I smiled in a satisfied, powerful kind of a way. "Good. Now pull the cover off the mattress and place it over here, in the big space on the floor at the end of the bed."

He did as I'd asked, moving on hands and knees to complete the task. It seemed strange to see my husband crawling. The muscles in his back rippled and the dip of his sweet arse cheeks sank. The sight made my pussy wet and my nipples peaked against their scratchy containment. He was truly beautiful.

"Good, now attach your left wrist to the leg of the bed." I dropped the handcuffs near him. "And hurry, we don't have all day."

Oh, we so did! Today and tomorrow.

Metal clicked and Jacob sat with his left arm extended, handcuff fixed tight.

"Lie completely flat on the floor," I said, holding up the other set of handcuffs, the pair that would render him completely at my mercy.

He shuffled down, and I moved swiftly to secure his other arm then stood, straight and proud, and looked down at the perfect specimen of a man I'd caught for myself.

His eyelids were heavy, his mouth slightly parted. His chest rose and fell quickly, as if he'd been doing something strenuous in the garden. His arms were raised high, the same way he'd tied me to the trees in the woods. The delicate skin of his underarm, coated in coal-black silken hair, was exposed; as was the outline of his ribs as his torso stretched long and lean.

The dark hair over his chest continued down his taut abs to his cock, where the strands were bushy and thick and wiry. His engorged dick pointed to the ceiling, the head swollen and the slit wide. I could imagine how firm and hot it would feel in my hands. How it would be like silk on steel, satin on iron. I loved his cock. I loved Jacob with every beat of my heart, and I loved his cock too.

His legs were together, the thick hairs on his thighs tapering off at his knees then becoming increasingly dense on his shins. His feet were tipped slightly outwards, his long toes and the arch of his foot vulnerable and pale.

"Spread your legs," I instructed, pacing to the desk at the end of the long room.

I could feel his gaze burning into my body as I reached for the wooden, straight-backed chair.

"Wider," I said.

He stretched his legs further apart until he was lying in a star shape.

"Good," I said, placing the chair on the floor between his lower limbs, the front legs just above his knees. Jacob had said one of the things that turned him on about being tied up was not being able to touch me—to lay there wanting me, needing me, but unable to do anything about it. I'd thought about this a lot and was looking forward to giving him quite a show. In fact, my clit was already buzzing for it to begin.

I retrieved the flogger then stepped over him, placing one foot either side of his chest.

"You may look at my pussy," I said, stooping slightly and trailing the flogger over his face and down the column of his throat. "In fact, you're not to take your attention from my pussy until I give you permission."

Carefully stepping backwards on my spiked heels, I sat on the chair with my legs stretched wide apart, the heels of my boots pressed into the carpet outside of his thighs.

"I know you want to look at my pussy," I said in a low voice as I ran the tails of the flogger up my thigh and over my bare, exposed cunt. "You like looking at my pussy and you like touching my pussy, don't you, Jacob?"

There was a rise of colour on his cheekbones as he nodded and pressed his lips together. He seemed mesmerised by the trailing tails of the flogger caressing my engorged lips.

A glut of power seared through me. Power and pleasure. Seeing Jacob so aroused and willing to get into a role he'd initially been nervous about told me I was doing it right. I'd taken control and he was enjoying relinquishing it.

I began to finger myself, rolling and toying with my clit and dipping into my entrance. I was wet and hot and craving more. "You know what I think of when I masturbate, Jacob?" I asked.

He swallowed tightly and shook his head, never once taking his gaze from my exploring, busy fingers.

"When you're at work and I'm horny, or, if you're away on business, I have no choice but to touch myself. But it's always you. I always think of you and your glorious, big cock."

Turning the flogger around, I touched the tip of the handle to my entrance. "I love the way you fuck me with your cock, Jacob. The fact that you hover, just for a split second, before you plunge in." After rotating the leather head around the rim of my pussy to gather natural lube, I eased it in. "Oh, God, Jacob, you always feel so big and hard. And hot, you always feel so hot when you sink into me."

Scooting to the edge of the chair so I could tilt my pelvis, I slid the handle in higher. I caught my breath and squeezed my eyes shut. It felt cool and hard, and although not as big as Jacob's girth, it was still a very satisfying entry.

"Do you like watching my pussy getting fucked?" I gasped, setting up a steady in-out rhythm.

Silence, except for the sound of my moisture clicking around the handle.

"Speak, you can speak," I snapped.

"Yes, yes I like it, you look so fucking horny, so fucking swollen and turned on."

"And you want to fuck me, don't you? When I'm turned on and wet and swollen you want to sink your big, fat cock into me, don't you? Ram in fast and hard and hear me cry out. Don't you, Jacob? Answer me."

"Yes. Yes."

"But you can't, you're tied up, on the floor. The flogger is fucking me..." I paused and sought my clit with my other hand. "The flogger is going to make me come while you watch. That is all you can do, watch—watch me get fucked."

My heart rate picked up and a feverish flush crawled over my skin. The domed handle rubbed over my G-spot, hitting just the right spot and, combined with stimulation over my engorged clit, it wouldn't be long until Jacob got to witness my orgasm.

"Ah, ah, yes, yes," I hissed, opening my eyes and looking down at his face.

It took a second to focus on his rapt expression, but when I did a thrilling whack of satisfaction reeled through me. He was loving my show.

"Jacob, oh, God, I always think of you, you and your dick. Whenever I touch myself I always think of you touching me, always you, only you." My toes curled in my boots, my legs tensed.

He too was panting, and a glance at his straining cock revealed a pearly drip of pre-cum sitting in his slit.

"I'm coming, Jacob, watch me come, I order you...to watch...me...come."

I was there. With several fast, furious thrusts of the handle and deep pressure on my clit, I burst into a mass of pulsating ecstasy. "Oh, God, yes, so fucking good," I cried. "Jacob, speak, can you see me coming?"

"Yes, I can see you and I want to make you come again, now."

As the waves of bliss turned into ripples of pleasure I became aware of the clanking of handcuffs. He was twisting and turning, trying to get out of them.

"Oh, no you don't," I said, swiftly withdrawing the handle and standing even though my cunt was still spasming. "You have to lie there like a good boy and have what I decide you're allowed."

He stilled and looked up at me.

A trickle of moisture further dampened the inside of my thighs. My breath was hard to catch. "But as you've been good so far, you can have some of this." Still holding the flogger, I gripped the end of the bed, a panel of straight, polished wood, and squatted down over his face.

"Can you see my cum?" I asked.

"Yes, you're soaked with it."

"I know, and I'm going to let you lick it off." I sank lower, so I was positioned wide and open over his face.

He let out a low growl and strained upwards to meet my pussy.

"Oh, yes, that's it," I groaned as he gave a gentle lick over the whole length of my lips. "That's it," I said in a soft voice. "Taste my juices, taste my cunt."

He set up a hungry, methodical system of lapping and delving, sucking and slurping. Whenever he was too firm over my super-sensitive clit I raised a little, eliciting moans of frustration from him.

Eventually, as my breathing returned to normal, I lifted up again. My pussy hummed nicely with satisfaction as I moved the chair out of our way.

"You really are behaving very well," I said, lying down over him, again being careful with my heels. "You can stop looking at my cunt now, I think you deserve another reward." I kissed him—hot, hard and open-mouthed. The way he kissed me when he was getting impatient for action. When I knew it wouldn't be long until he was thrusting inside me.

He tasted of me, of my cum and my cunt, his tongue slippery as it tangled with mine.

Breaking the kiss, I headed lower, sweeping my lips around his tight, dark nipples, then biting them lightly.

He groaned and a tremble travelled through his body.

Kneeling between his legs, I used the strands of the flogger as I continued on my downward journey, tickling over his abs and hips and finally his cock.

"Your dick is very hard, Jacob," I said, swiping the top of his thighs with the flogger. Not enough to inflict pain, but enough to make him wonder what I would do next. "Would you like me to suck your dick?"

Silence.

"You may speak."

"Yes, oh, God, yes, Karen, suck my dick, please."

I chuckled at his desperate voice and discarded the flogger. I would need both my hands for this next bit. Taking his shaft in my fist, I circled the head of his cock, spreading the pre-cum over it and around the ridge of his glans.

He twisted his neck and gritted his teeth. I would have to play it careful. It wouldn't take much to make him come, and we were nowhere near ready for that point yet.

Dipping my head, I swiped my tongue over his glans then took him halfway into my mouth.

He groaned, long and loud, tensed his thighs around me.

I sank lower, slowly, carefully taking him deep, right to the back of my throat. Once he was nestled there I set up a small gulping action with the base of my tongue.

He released a colourful string of expletives and another drip of pre-cum dampened my palate.

I would have liked to suck on his cock for longer, but he was too close. So I lifted up from his shaft and took it in my palm. "You are going to have to trust me for this next bit, Jacob."

"Oh, God, don't stop," he moaned, his eyes tight shut.

"It's going to get a whole lot better in a minute, but you have to trust me the way I have trusted you plenty of times."

Silence.

"Do you trust me, Jacob? Speak."

"Yes, yes of course."

"You remember our safe word?"

"Yes." He opened his eyes. They were heavy and dark as if drugged.

Standing again, I reached for the bag. From it I withdrew

a small, purple butt plug and a tube of lube.

"Oh, fuck," he said, his narrowed eyes suddenly widening.

"You can either trust me to make you feel amazing or you can say the safe word, Jacob. What is it going to be?"

He juddered in a breath. Tried to move his arms and succeeded only in rattling the handcuffs on the bed's legs.

"I'll take that as a 'you want to feel amazing'," I said, sinking down between his legs, placing the plug and lube on the sheet next to me and taking a gentle but firm hold of his cock.

"Oh, God," he murmured, pressing his face into the upstretched ball of his shoulder and exposing his gritted teeth.

"Shh," I soothed, rubbing up and down his shaft. "Shh, it's going to be good. I know it is." My voice was calming, but inside I was a bundle of excitement. Bloody hell, he really was going to let me insert the butt plug. When I'd bought it for him I'd had visions of him telling me I'd gone crazy and refusing it totally. But although I'd surprised him, he was up for me inserting things into *his* body for a change.

As I stroked his shaft with one hand I used the other to fondle his balls. I knew he liked that and it would relax him. The butt plug wasn't big, but nor had it been the smallest in the shop. I needed to slow him down a bit, release some of the tension I'd built up.

I nudged his legs a little wider with my knees, pulled his sac up slightly and revealed his tightly puckered hole. It was the first time I'd seen his anus with the thought of touching it, penetrating it.

For a moment I just stared.

Then, letting go of him, I reached for the plug once more. My heart raced, my stomach in a frenzy of anticipation as I coated the purple toy in clear lube.

"Just relax, Jacob, this feels amazing, even more so for a guy, you just wait and see."

He replied with a fragmented groan as I touched the cool, tapered tip to his anus.

"Shh," I said again and gave a gentle nudge—it seemed impossible that the plug would press in. His ring was clasped so tight. "Jacob," I whispered. "Let me in the way I let you into my body."

A tremble rattled over his torso, and he let out a long, slow breath. I felt his arse give a tiny bit and pushed the plug in with a more determined pressure.

"Oh, fuck," he said, his body jerking.

"It's okay, that's the hardest bit," I soothed. "Now just relax."

He yanked his arms and the cuffs banged wildly. There was only one thing for it. I took his cock in my mouth and sank down.

"Oh, Jesus, heaven help me," he gasped, stilling all movement.

As I hit maximum depth on his cock I eased the plug in some more. It glided in easily now, the lube smoothing the way as he relaxed.

I scraped my teeth along his shaft, lifted up and released his cock. I looked at the plug penetrating him. "You've nearly taken it all," I said, pulling the smooth toy almost out then easing it back in again.

He groaned, low and guttural, his eyes shut tight and the cords on his neck strained.

My pussy was on fire. Never in my wildest dreams had I thought tying Jacob up and inserting something into him would be so erotic. But it was. It was an act that required him to trust me one hundred per cent. An act so brazen and forbidden that I knew we'd never tell anyone else about it, not for as long as we both lived.

"Does it feel good? Tell me, Jacob," I asked, repeating my gentle thrusting movements over and over. Fucking his arse with the toy.

"Good, I dunno, weird…kind of full and burning. Touching something which has never been touched."

"Yes, I know." And I also knew that if I tipped the base of the plug towards the floor the end would press on his prostate. That would, according to the internet, feel amazing for him—a bit like when he hit my G-spot.

He twitched his hips with each long glide I treated him to, and his cock bobbed. He was taking it well and had grown used to the invasion.

It was time.

Firmly dipping the base of the plug, I popped it completely into his anus so only the small arms remained outside.

"Argh, oh, fuck..."

"Shh, it's okay." Quickly, I straddled him. Positioned my pussy over his cock and sat down, taking his hard length deep into my wet channel. "I'm going to fuck you now, Jacob, and you can come; you can come when you need to."

"Karen, Karen, I..." His words tailed off, his body bucked beneath mine, and the bed shifted, his fractious, frantic arms exerting considerable force on the furniture.

Quickly, I undid the halter at the nape of my neck and let it fall down. My breasts hung free and swung wildly as I picked up a rapid pace. Grinding myself onto his cock and thrusting my clit into his hairy pubis.

"Look at me, look at me fucking you," I ordered.

He peeled open his eyes and stared up at my jostling breasts.

"I'm fucking you so hard," I panted. "I'm going to make you come like never before, Jacob."

Briefly, it crossed my mind that I really should have tied his legs down too. He was bucking beneath me. Shifting and arching, rising to meet my thrusts, the handcuffs barely containing his writhing body.

We were banging and crashing. The sound of flesh slapping against flesh combined with the groaning strains of the wooden bedframe created quite a din.

"Ah, yes, yes, come!" I yelled, knotting my fingers in my hair and throwing back my head. "Come, come with me."

"Argh, oh, Jesus, fucking hell," he cried.

As I spiralled into a wondrous series of convulsions, he thrust and pumped into me.

"Karen, oh God, what have you done?" he howled.

I was still coming, eking out the heavenly orgasm swamping me. Knowing what I'd created deep inside Jacob's most private place added momentum to an already mind-blowing crescendo.

"Oh, fuck, that…is…it!" he shouted.

Warmth flooded my pussy.

"Oh, Jacob," I managed, dropping over him, my breasts pressing into his chest. "Oh, God, that was amazing."

He grunted.

"You can talk," I said breathlessly.

"I can't," he said with a panting gasp, "I think you've finished me off."

I touched my lips to his. "Don't be so dramatic."

His glazed eyes snared mine. "I think you ought to get that thing out of me, or uncuff me so I can do it."

Quickly, I lifted off his cock and slithered down his body. It only took a second to remove the plug and toss it aside, then I was back over him.

"I want to hold you," he said, tugging his arms.

"In a minute." I grinned, wickedly. "Once you've told me exactly how you thought I did at acting out your fantasy." We were still both breathing quickly.

"It was good."

"Just good?"

"Great."

I tipped my head and pushed several sweat-damp strands of hair from my cheek. Frowned slightly.

"Do we have to analyse it?" he asked.

"No, not at all. I just want some feedback."

"Okay, well that was one hell of an intense orgasm."

"Good." I narrowed my eyes. "But what?" I knew he was holding something back.

"But, does that make me gay, that I liked that, you know, up my arse?"

I laughed. "No, of course not. It was *me* doing it to you, not another guy."

He smiled, a little. "You sure?"

"Absolutely. Lots of married couples play around like that, male and female married couples."

His shoulders relaxed as much as they could in their binds, then, "How do *you* know?"

"I looked it up on the internet."

His loud guffaw filled the room. "You and the bloody internet."

I laughed with him then said, "Happy anniversary."

Chapter Eleven

The next morning, I woke expecting Jacob to still be flaked out beside me, but he was sitting on the chair I'd occupied between his legs the night before and dressed, ready for the day. Quick-fire fast, the memories flooded my mind, and I allowed myself an indulgent smile. It had gone well, hadn't it? Just as I'd hoped it would. I admitted his lack of wanting to share his true inner feelings about the experience had… pinched a little. Yes, it had pinched, but not enough for it to sour my mood or for me to want to ponder on it too much. Maybe he needed time to digest it, to accept that he wasn't a pervert for enjoying what we'd done. God knows I'd been through the same sort of thing.

Once he'd fully accepted that what we did remained between us, he'd be okay. God, it wasn't like I had a close enough friend to tell anyway, and I knew damn well he wouldn't share our experiences with anyone at work. He always said he liked to keep his private and work lives separate, never allowing those he worked with to know anything but the basics about us.

He smiled at me, mug in hand—coffee if the scents coming my way were anything to go by—and my tummy did somersaults. He was okay, happy, and that was all I needed to know.

"Morning, love," he said, as he walked over to me, his dark jeans rustling in the quiet. He planted a soft kiss on the top of my head and trailed the backs of his fingers down my cheek.

I closed my eyes and breathed in the fresh, clean smell of him. He'd showered. And, of course, the thought that

I didn't look my best in the morning sprang to mind, me imagining what he saw—hair a tangled riot, face lined from being squashed against the pillow, sleepy dust in the corners of my eyes. I stretched, rubbed that dust away with my fists, and stifled a yawn. "Morning. You woke early."

"Yep. Thought we should take advantage of the breakfast on offer. Or maybe we could go out for some. Find a little cafe. Whatever you like."

He moved to a small mahogany sideboard that held a kettle and the paraphernalia for making tea or coffee, and switched on the kettle, which took only a few seconds to re-boil. I watched him make me some tea, taking in the sight of his muscles as they moved beneath his thin, white cotton shirt, shoulder blades that jutted, biceps that bunched. I was greedy to touch him all over, to have him strip, get back into bed, and make slow love to me.

"This'll wake you up a bit." He glanced at his watch as he brought the mug over, steam writhing from the top, white and thick like mist. "Then you can shower and we'll get our day started."

I sat up, took the mug, and patted the space beside me. He sat, knees apart, hands dangling between them. I noticed chafe marks, pink rings around his wrists, some areas darker than others, especially where the knobble of bone protruded. He rubbed them, trying hard to hide a wince.

"Sore?" I asked. Anxious over what his answer would be, I took a sip of tea—tea that didn't taste the same as it did at home—and hoped for the best.

"A bit, but a good kind of sore." He turned his head, smiled, then allowed that smile to spread into an outright grin.

Relieved, I smiled back. "I know what you mean. It's something different, isn't it? And we don't have to do that again if you don't want to."

"I do," he said quickly. "I loved it. Loved you, the way you were." He linked his fingers, unlocked them, seemingly unsure what to do with himself.

Was he embarrassed?

"Listen," I said, thinking it best to change the subject. "What will we do today? What d'you fancy?"

He grinned again, looked from me to his wrists and back again, a sparkle in his eyes. God, he *had* loved it.

"No idea," he said, as though that look hadn't told me exactly what was on his mind. "Though I do think we ought to see a bit more of this place. Going home tomorrow. It'd be nice to pick up some souvenirs for the girls. We could do that then come back here..."

"All right."

I drank my tea as quickly as I could, suddenly hungry for a big breakfast that would set me up for the day. I showered, dressed, and within half an hour of waking up we were down in the hotel restaurant, sampling Amsterdam's version of a full English breakfast. Okay, the chef had tried, I'd give him that, but it just wasn't the same. The sausages weren't anything like our bangers—more like hotdogs—and the scrambled eggs were runny, reminding me of cottage cheese. Still, it filled a hole, and as we walked into the lobby, my belly pushing against the waistband of my jeans, I spotted a crowd gathering.

"Wonder what's going on?" I said.

Instead of answering, Jacob went over and asked, returning with a smile and a zest for life in his eyes. "It's one of those tour things, but not the boring kind. You get to visit all the places the locals go to, and today is this big open-air market. Want to go?"

I did, and Jacob looked buoyed by the idea—it wasn't every weekend we were in Amsterdam, was it? Not like we could do this some other time in the near future. I liked open-air markets as much as he did, so while Jacob went to the desk to buy our bus tickets, I dashed back to our room to collect coats, my bag, and the camera. The weather here was much the same as at home, and if it got a bit chilly as we browsed we could buy some cheap gloves.

I returned to the lobby just in time. The crowd had

filed outside, forming a disjointed line alongside the bus, clapping their hands owing to the cold and stamping their feet. We'd definitely need to buy gloves. Jacob waited beside the door, and together we tagged onto the end of the queue, me feeling ridiculously excited at doing something off the cuff. And why shouldn't we? With no one to answer to, no demands on our time, we could do what the bloody hell we pleased.

It felt good.

The journey would take around half an hour, so I began to while away the time listening to the various languages and accents of the others on board. Jacob looked out of the window as I people-watched, studying the scenery as it zipped by. One woman, aged about sixty, sat beside her husband of around the same age, her hand held tightly in his. I thought of me and Jacob in the future, how we'd take holidays together more regularly once the girls had left home. How, when we were the same age as that couple, we'd still hold hands too. Unlike when we were younger and thought older people having sex was disgusting, I stared at the elderly lovers and felt only admiration that their love still held strong after probably spending years together already. I wanted us to be like them in years to come, and we would, I had no doubt about that.

I reached over and took Jacob's hand in mine. Squeezed it.

"What?" he asked, turning from the window to look at me.

"Nothing."

"So why the squeeze?"

He knew why, we did it often enough, but I answered him anyway.

"I just love you, that's all. Felt the need to show it." I stared ahead at the back of the seat in front, small smile playing about my mouth.

"Ten years yesterday, love. It's gone quick, hasn't it?" He stroked my hand with his thumb.

"It has. Imagine another ten."

"Another twenty."

I squeezed his hand again. "We'll make it to fifty."

"You reckon?"

I stared at him sharply, but upon seeing the grin filling the bottom half of his face I realised he'd said it to wind me up. I playfully slapped him then rested my cheek against his arm.

"I reckon we'll make it," I said, my voice full of conviction. "How can we not when we feel like this?"

For the remainder of the journey, I closed my eyes and watched scenarios from that book playing out in my mind – except I orchestrated the way they went to make the fantasy completely mine. I smiled at the results.

We arrived at the market in no time – typical, when I'd found a way to amuse myself – and as the bus lurched to a stop, I stood and stretched. People filed off, dispersing into the crowd, soon gone from sight among the many bobble-hatted people getting off other buses and streaming from cars.

I wasn't prepared for the size of the market. It would take all day to get around. No wonder the bus driver had said he'd return at four. Rows and rows of tarpaulin-covered stalls – some white, some blue-striped, some red – stretched on forever, and I glanced at Jacob to see whether we'd made a mistake.

"Fuck me, look at the size of this place!" he said, his voice animated, eyebrows high curves of surprise.

"Massive, isn't it?" I said, itching to delve into the regimented rows and see what an Amsterdam market had to offer.

Four hours later, thoroughly exhausted but happy, we came to the final row. Earlier, we'd bought the girls a few bits and bobs, small items that would fit in our case and not take the weight up too much, but I hadn't seen anything that called out to me, made me want to buy it. We walked on, our pace slower than it had been at the start, and I noticed one stall had rather a large gathering waiting to peruse its goods. As we approached, I tugged Jacob's arm and led him to the side of the throng, my curiosity piqued as to what had attracted so many people. I leaned over, peered through the bodies—and caught a glimpse of a row of vibrators. What the hell? I knew the good people of Amsterdam were more liberal than us British, but bloody hell!

My cheeks heated. "It's a bloody sex stall!" I whispered, eyes wide.

"Fucking hell! Really? On a market?"

"Yes!" I hissed. "I'm going to take a look!"

"Jesus, Karen!" He glanced about nervously.

"What? We don't *know* anyone here. Come on, it'll be funny."

Spotting a break in the crowd, I surged forward and yanked Jacob along behind me. The deep tented area was large, rows of tables set out horizontally, the aisles between them packed with people. I gripped Jacob's hand so I wouldn't lose him. It was slow going, shuffling one step at a time to view the items for sale, but God, it was worth it. I wanted to buy everything, but with no room in my case I'd have to buy all these things over the internet once we got home.

"Will you look at *that?*" Jacob said, pointing to a long, thick butt plug with bobbles all over it. "Pleasure or pain?" he whispered.

I thought about it. "Pain, until you got used to it. Those balls would rub your—"

"All right, all right," he said, darting his gaze about again.

"Oh, stop being so paranoid. No one here gives a shit!"

As the butt plugs gave way to love balls and clitoral stimulators, further up I spied piles of books. It took a couple of minutes to reach them, but they left me in no doubt as to what they contained. Their covers were explicit, and just the sight of men and women in various sexual poses made my cunt clench. I wanted one of the books so badly, just to look at when Jacob was away at work, and, if I was honest, to give me ideas.

I shuffled through them, soaking up the sexiness, my face heated by a hot blush. Not of embarrassment, but of arousal. Thank God the bus would be leaving soon. I couldn't wait to get back to our hotel. I glanced sideways at Jacob, whose eyes were wide, his mouth curved into a secret smile, then continued my perusal. I found one that was just pictures, a *Karma Sutra* using real people, cocks and cunts on show. I studied them, aroused by the sight of the large erections and glistening labia, and glanced at Jacob's midsection. It left me in no doubt that he was aroused too. Once I'd reached the last page, I searched for other, similar books. My assault on them was so vigorous, I knocked one pile over. They fanned out over the others, the corner of one making my mouth go dry and my heartbeat flutter erratically. It couldn't be, could it?

I reached out, slid the book free.

"Oh my God, it's that filthy book!" I shrieked, clamping my mouth shut as people turned to stare my way. I clutched the book to my chest, memories of having read it steam-rolling into my mind.

"Filthy book?" Jacob asked.

"Um, yes. I read it a long time ago. Before I met you."

"Let me see."

He reached out to take it, but with an odd, fiercely protective streak, I wouldn't let him have it. It remained pinned against me, both my arms crossed over it.

"Karen?"

"Just…just give me a minute, will you?"

I was being irrational, I knew that, but with shame and embarrassment consuming me, I had to have a few seconds to process my feelings. That book, that deliciously filthy book, had been my first introduction to the more adventurous side of sex all those years ago. And now, these last few months, it had been where I'd got my fantasies from. The talking dirty, the rape scenario, being tied up. When those ideas had come to me, when we'd acted one of them out on our first weekend away, it had taken me a while to figure out where the hell they'd come from, but deep down I'd known damn well. I remembered feeling dirty after I'd read this book; that it was wrong somehow to be turned on by such things. The contents of those pages had followed me for days, weeks, months, years it seemed, and being as young as I was, when my friends still giggled at the idea of a boyfriend fumbling inside their knickers, that new knowledge had burnt.

Back then I'd vowed never to read it again, never even to think of it again.

When I'd left home to move in with Jacob, packing up my things had brought the book right to the forefront of my mind again. As I'd taken it out from under my mattress, my cheeks had grown hot, my stomach had bunched, and God, my cunt had flooded. I'd dared to look at it one last time, then shoved it into the bottom of a cardboard box, other books on top of it as if them being there would disguise it, and sealed the sod up tight with wide brown packing tape.

At Jacob's I'd climbed into the attic, hefting the box up there with me, and stowed it in a dark, far corner. By the time we'd moved again, to where we lived now, I'd forgotten all about it. Jacob had been in charge of shifting boxes around, while I'd made sure our girls, small as they were then, hadn't got into any mischief amongst the chaos.

Where the hell is that box now?

I slowly prised the book away from my body and stared down at it. The title was in Dutch, but I knew it said *My Erotic Fantasies*. Knew every damn word inside it. Knew that one fantasy had yet to be played out. It filled my mind, and my pussy throbbed, clit aching. I wondered if Jacob would be up for it, considering it was so out of the norm. Most people didn't do such things, did they? But then, we'd discovered lately we weren't most people…

Reluctantly I put the book down, took Jacob's hand, and despite his questioning look, pulled him over to a stall designed to look like a cafe. It was relatively empty, considering the number of people here, and I found us a table at the back, away from eavesdroppers. I had to explain—and find out where that cardboard box was.

I left him seated and went up to the steel counter. I ordered two coffees and a pastry each. Eating would give me something to do with my hands if I grew nervous. And I would be, because I'd never shared my reading that book with Jacob. Hell, I'd buried it deep inside my mind, forgotten about it, but as we'd begun to share things about ourselves we'd previously kept hidden, I'd begun to acknowledge where my ideas had come from. I felt I owed it to him to tell him I hadn't thought of them on my own.

Back at the table, I placed the scarred wooden tray down and sat opposite him on a white plastic patio chair, my stomach in knots. He wouldn't think me dirty, would he? Not after the things we'd been doing. Yet the old insecurities came back just the same. This was something I'd read when he wasn't in my life, and although I knew we couldn't help our pasts, it felt all kinds of wrong that I hadn't told him about it. I felt *guilty*, for God's sake!

"Look, if you don't want to tell me, it's okay," he said, sipping coffee from a polystyrene cup that became distorted in his grip, the rim squashed like a flat smile. "Bound to be things we did before we met that neither of us have talked about."

I broke my pastry in two. "Have you got any?"

"No, love, but I'm trying to make you feel better." He popped a sultana in his mouth.

"Oh." I felt worse. "I want to tell you because, well, it's a part of me I forgot about for many years, but it all makes sense—why I wanted to do the things we've done lately. It makes me feel better to tell you because I don't want you thinking I made the fantasies up. At first, I thought I had no idea where they'd come from, so I thought I was a raging pervert, but now I know I'm not because I got the ideas from that book and—"

"It's perfectly normal, love."

Jacob appeared unfazed, sipping again from his out-of-shape cup and eyeing me over the lip. Once again I was thankful I had him in my life. He understood absolutely everything.

"Men watch porn, right?" he said. "As a teenager I watched it whenever I could, I told you that. Doesn't make me weird, just your average kid. You giving me a blowjob," he lowered his voice a fraction after glancing around, "with me directing the pace—I saw that in a porno film and it stuck in my head. Turned me the fuck on, if I'm honest. But I never wanted to bring it up with you because most women don't like that kind of thing. And I didn't want you thinking I was some nasty bastard, know what I mean?" He paused to look at me, face flushed, eyes rapidly blinking. "And you reading that book doesn't make you weird either. It's natural."

"But at the time, those things were considered *not* normal. I never would have known people did that kind of thing if I hadn't read it. And now we're doing those things, I know they're not bad, but seeing that book again…"

"Has it brought the shame back?"

"It did at first, but now…" I took a deep breath. "Did you take everything out of the attic when we moved to our house?"

"Yes, love."

"Everything? I mean, even from the back corners?"

"Yes…"

"So, do you remember a red box of books kept closed with brown tape?"

"No, but I took everything to the new house, so if it was in the old attic, it'll be in ours now."

"Right. Good."

He widened his eyes. "Ah, that filthy book is in our attic, isn't it?"

I nodded. "Do you want to read it?"

"Damn right I do."

A frisson of excitement nipped my insides. "See, once

I saw the book again, I remembered something. There's this thing, something we could do. I used to think it was filthy, but these days… God, I want to try it out. I want to experience it. Even if it's only once."

"What is it?"

I glanced around the stall. No one was taking any notice of us, but I leant forward anyway. Whispered in Jacob's ear. Once I'd finished, he sat back, looking at me with the glint I'd so hoped would be there.

"You'd be willing to try that? In a place like that?"

"Would you?"

"Fuck, yes!"

"Shall we…"

"Yes. Yes."

* * * *

At the hotel, with Jacob lounging on the bed, I sat beside him, muddling through the telephone book at adverts for various places. I had no idea what most of them were for, the language being a huge barrier. Those that had pictures of tools or cups, scissors or houses were easy to work out, but I didn't think the kind of place we were after would have images beside them to help a person out. Maybe they weren't even *in* the telephone book.

I sighed, tapped my lower lip with a finger, and walked over to a sideboard similar to the one with the kettle on it. The hotel provided internet access, and a netbook sat waiting for me to boot it up. Okay, it was firmly fixed onto the sideboard with some metal struts so no one could steal it, and I preferred browsing online in comfort, but I wasn't about to complain. I hunched over it and Googled, finding the information we needed in an instant. A place like the one we sought was only two streets away, and I wondered if it would look seedy on the outside or be nondescript, hiding the delights it offered inside.

"I've found one," I said, looking over my shoulder.

Jacob shot off the bed and stood behind me, peering at the screen over my shoulder. "Fuck, we're really going to do it, aren't we?"

I craned my neck to look at him. "We can always back out. Think about it some more. Plan the evening and find a similar place when we get home."

"No." He shook his head. "We're anonymous here. It's better this way."

"All right," I said, scribbling down the telephone number, logging off then snapping the netbook shut. "Are you ringing them or shall I? We've got to hope they're not booked up." My stomach rolled so violently I thought I might be sick.

"You do it. It's your fantasy." He scrubbed his chin, the day's growth of stubble rasping, and winked.

"Okay." I picked up the phone and dialled the fetish sex club.

Chapter Twelve

We stood, hand in hand, outside Club Nirvana, staring at the glossy black door and the wide window drawn with red velvet curtains. It said on the website that the exclusive venue was for sexually curious individuals and broad-minded couples – we guessed we fell into both those categories by now.

"You still up for it?" Jacob asked, his voice and face animated by both apprehension and excitement.

"Yes, absolutely."

And I was, but God, my heart was beating wildly. I was up for the exhilaration, of doing something I'd never thought I would do in my wildest dreams, yet needle jabs of anxiety brought goosebumps out all over my body.

Think of the book, what the author said it feels like…

I took a deep breath and stepped forward, my silver spiked heels loud on the cold pavement. There was no reason not to go in. This was something we both wanted. It was risk free, as far as we could tell, and fate seemed to have once again blown circumstances our way.

When I'd spoken to a lady on the phone, who'd had perfect English, she'd said that as a rule it was a members only club, but for the entire month they were having a special discounted 'one night only' offer. Not only that, but when I'd enquired about the *kamer voyeuristische* – oh my bloody good God, a voyeuristic room! – she'd announced it was free at nine o'clock that very evening, our last night in Amsterdam, and the only rule was that we had to be attired in fetish wear.

I was fine with the rule after my shopping spree the day

before, but we'd been stuck for Jacob. In the end we'd had no choice but to splurge some cash on a pair of black leather trousers. Hardly hardcore fetish, but I figured with his top off and another addition I was hoping to find in the club shop, he would look the part.

The door opened into a plush reception. Ruby red walls, deep, well-worn sofas and a chandelier hanging from the ceiling.

"*Hallo,*" a dark-haired woman said, looking up from a desk that held an enormous vase of red roses.

"Er, hello," I said. "We have the *kamer voyeuristische* booked for nine."

She smiled. "Ah, yes, Karen and Jacob, correct?"

I nodded.

"It is great to have you in Amsterdam and at Club Nirvana. I hope you have a wonderful time with us. The rules are simple. Respect and consent." She glanced at our linked hands. "Though I am sure you already live by that rule."

"Yes," I said, squeezing Jacob's fingers.

"You are a little early. The room is still being prepared for you. Would you like to peruse the shop first? Perhaps see if there are any more toys you would like to purchase? Viewers always like to see toys."

"Yes," Jacob said quickly.

I looked up at him.

He caught my eye. "What? We do want to look in the shop, we've only brought one thing."

"Yes, yes we do, you're right."

The woman smiled and led us down a narrow corridor. It smelt of perfume and cigarette smoke. The walls held photographs of exposed pussies and erect cocks, and I would like to have stopped and stared, but there was no time, not if we wanted to look in the shop.

"After your time in *kamer voyeuristische,* feel free to go to the bar for a drink. Later on there is a medical show." She turned and smiled. "Tonight is my debut. I'm playing the nurse who administers the enema."

"Sounds interesting," Jacob said, and although he tried to hide it I could hear a note of disbelief in his voice.

"It is." She stopped outside a closed door, turned to Jacob and gave him the once-over, right from his black boots up to his rugged, should've-shaved jawline. There was approval in her eyes, as though she liked the look of him and wouldn't mind stripping him naked and doing strange enema things to his body.

I reached for his hand again and pressed my shoulder into his arm.

She tilted her chin and sighed, almost wistfully. "Here is the shop. They take credit cards, and this door opposite leads you along a passageway to the *kamer voyeuristische.* At nine o'clock on the dot it will be ready for you. At two minutes past you will be on show. You have forty minutes booked. Please note we have security cameras overseeing all activities in the establishment. Do not worry, they are discarded later if nothing untoward occurs, but if you wish to have a DVD of your time in *kamer voyeuristische*, that can be arranged. You will need to attend to your bill on the way out." She swept her tongue over her glossy red lips and settled a sultry gaze on Jacob. "Have fun."

"Er, yes, thanks," he said.

She stalked away, her hips rolling.

After a brief hesitation, Jacob pushed the door to the shop open.

Ten minutes later and one hundred euros lighter—four purchases, none of which would be souvenirs for the mantelpiece—we made our way through the second door we'd been directed to use.

It was almost nine.

In the distance I could hear music. It wasn't thumping, it was languid and jazzy. I imagined it coming from a smoky bar where a girl twirled around a silver pole, nipple tassels swinging, crotch bared whenever her legs parted.

My nerves started to mount now that the practicalities

were seen to. Could I really do this? How would it feel? What if I hated it? What if Jacob hated it?

"You okay, love?" Jacob asked, resting his hand on my shoulder as we walked.

"Yes, yes I'm fine."

"You still want me to take control or do you want to again, like you did last night?"

I stopped at the single heavy door at the end of the corridor and placed our bag of purchases on a table.

"I still want you to take control," I said, turning to him. "You've had more practice at it than me."

He grinned. "Yeah, I suppose that's true." He set our bag from the hotel onto the table and pulled me into his arms. "And I've loved every minute of it, just like I know we're going to enjoy this too, the final chapter in that filthy book of yours." He kissed me, hotly, deeply, thoroughly, and I melted into him. I wouldn't have been completely opposed to taking control this evening, but I didn't, in my heart of hearts, believe Jacob was ready for it. Last night had been his first submission, his first time allowing me to invade his body. We needed more private time to settle into that new way of being together.

He pulled back from our kiss and undid the buttons on my jacket. Smiled as he slipped it off and revealed my tight corset, fishnet-covered breasts and slip of a thong.

"You look stunning," he said, his pupils dilating. "Absolutely every horny dream and fantasy I've ever had has been about you, who you are and who you've become. I love you so much."

Warmth flooded my soul—and my pussy. "I love you too. I could only do this with you."

"I know, me too."

I smiled, took a deep breath and reached into the bag at my side. As Jacob shrugged out of his jacket and pulled off his jumper, I handed him the final piece of his outfit.

Just holding it made my nerves skitter. I knew it would. The material was soft, like the ski mask, but it was thicker, heavier, and when Jacob slid it over his head and down his face there was something obscenely sexual about it as well as menacing. His eyes looked as if they were permanently narrowed as he peered through the slits, his nose hidden right to the tip. The long black sides of the mask covered his cheeks, jawline and halfway down his neck. It was impossible to make out what colour or style his hair was.

"Does it suit me?" he asked.

I suppressed a delicious tremble. "Yes, very much."

"Good."

As I smoothed my stockings and rubbed away a scuff on my boots, he shifted a few purchases in the bag, tore wrappers, and the scent of a sterilising wipe hit my nose.

"It's show time," he said after a couple of minutes.

Blood thumped loud in my ears, and my stomach somersaulted. I fluffed my hair, rolled my lips in on themselves, and swallowed a bite of nerves. This was it, a once-in-a-lifetime opportunity. I had to make the most of it.

The *kamer voyeuristische* was oval shaped, the floor black tiled, the walls the same ruby red as the reception. In the middle stood a bench; a black leather, surgical-style bench. It had high, solid stirrups and long steel legs. A tray-like table on wheels waited next to it. But my concentration didn't linger on the bench I was about to be fucked on. Instead, I stared at the short black curtains circling the walls. Behind each, so the website had said, there was a window—a window that was designed especially for looking into this room, for watching the show.

And tonight it was to be our show, our debut performance. The Karen and Jacob Get-Down-and-Dirty show.

"It certainly seems clean and serviceable," Jacob said, walking swiftly to the table and laying out our equipment. Some items clinked, metal on metal, as he placed them down.

I glanced at a large round clock on the wall. We had two minutes until the curtains opened and our audience would gawp in. I pulled in a breath, my stomach clenched, and my pelvis seemed to actually hum with anticipation.

"Come here," Jacob said, holding out his hand. "It's time to get you ready and get in role."

I nodded and stepped up to him, melted against the hot, bare flesh of his chest. His kiss was firm and confident, his hands on my back sure and steady. In that moment, with that kiss, I knew everything would be okay. Jacob had it all covered.

We must have kissed for longer than I thought because it was the whirring of the electric motor opening the curtains that got my attention. We pulled apart, and as we did so there was a shift in the dynamics between us.

Jacob peered down at me through the slits in his mask. He placed his hands on my shoulders and urged me to turn.

As I moved I was aware of faces in windows. Round faces, round eyes, dimly lit features strewn with shadows.

A huge glut of excitement swamped me. These people were all here to see us, to watch what we did, how we had sex. They may even be sat there now, wondering what we'd look like when we were at it.

They were interested, they were curious, they were voyeuristic.

And they would soon find out what they wanted to know.

Jacob moved to the table, retrieved one of our recent purchases, and stood back behind me. He extended his arms over my shoulders and held it in front of my face.

I stared at the smooth, shiny ball and the thin leather strap. It was for me to wear. It would take away my voice, my safe word. It would show our audience how much I trusted my Master.

Opening my mouth, I studied the face of a middle-aged man in the window directly in front of me. He had a receding hairline, glasses, and wore a shirt and tie. He held my gaze as Jacob fastened the strap around the back of my head. Tight—tight enough to keep the gag ball in place and my jaw stretched.

The next thing I knew, Jacob was kneeling before me,

nuzzling my breasts through the netting. He sucked hard and fast, and I rested my hands on his material-covered head, swayed a little as the acute suction pinched deliciously. We'd talked about what we were going to do for our performance, but it wasn't an exact plan, only the bare bones had been agreed.

The rest was up to him.

Just as I thought my nipples were going to tear through the fishnet, Jacob stood and urged me to turn again, as if showing me off to a different set of windows. The man in the suit and tie would now have a good view of my ample rump.

Jaw stretched wide and my tongue pressing on the ball, I peered through a window at a young couple, male and female, with heavily pierced faces and gothic, black hair. They sat very still, clearly fascinated by us. I wondered if it was their first time watching.

Jacob fiddled with the knot at my nape then released the halter part of my top, exposing my breasts to the audience. I had a brief bout of self-consciousness. I hadn't shown the secret places of my body to anyone else in years.

But we don't know them. It doesn't matter.

He flicked and pinched, pulling each nipple to hard points. I let out a small groan, throaty and muted around the round lump of plastic in my mouth.

For a second he left me to go the table, and while he was gone I studied the woman behind the next window. She was elegant, her hair in a stylish up-do and a string of pearls around her neck. She tilted her chin when she saw my gaze had landed on her.

Jacob was back and dropped to his knees. With a swiftness that surprised me, he attached the first nipple clamp. It bit and tugged, nipped the engorged bud to a point of pain. I was just about to pull it off, instinct demanding it be removed, when he planted his mouth over the rise of my breast and spread warm, soothing kisses over my flesh. I remembered how I'd switched pain to pleasure when he'd beaten me in the woods. How I'd used the endorphins to give me an almighty high. It had been well worth the initial hurt.

Willing myself still, I tipped my head to the ceiling, shut my eyes, and allowed him to attach the other clamp, this time harnessing the sensations and letting the hot fingers of pain spread down to my pussy and poke at my clit.

"My God, your tits look incredible," he murmured, standing and sliding a hand between my legs.

I pressed into him, the swollen pain of my nipple points connecting with his hot chest.

He slipped his fingers to my clit, and I whimpered. I needed him to touch me so badly. I needed his skilful ministrations. I needed to come, soon, so I could revel in the tightness of the clamps as I built to orgasm. But, of course, I couldn't tell him that, couldn't demand a climax, not now, not with the ball gag in place.

"Mmm, you're hot and wet," he said, removing his finger and smoothing it through the roll of his tongue, deep into his mouth. "And you taste delicious."

I stared at his lips – it was the only thing I could really see on his face. He licked them exaggeratedly then smiled in a sinful, wicked way.

"Show everyone what you look like, whore. Show them your tortured tits and your slutty, crotchless knickers." He took my hand and led me to the side of the room, near to the windows.

My hips rolled as I walked, and the tops of my thighs slipped glassily against one another. I was so wet for Jacob, so turned on. Eager for him to get on with the main event. But it seemed he was going to prolong my agony.

As faces peered at me, I was sure people could feel my erotically charged state through the glass. My breasts swung, nipples growing heavier and more engorged by the second. My clit trembled with every tiny bit of friction walking created. If I hadn't been so hugely excited I would have felt bad that I couldn't smile at my audience, but I didn't care, and it didn't matter. They weren't there to see me being polite, they were there to see me get fucked. Fucked by the big masked man who had lots of tools of the trade to ensure that I had an amazing time.

Eventually, Jacob led me to the bench in the middle of the room. The faces in the windows had all blurred into one—it was just lots of eyes, lots of fascinated expressions, lots of minds about to be filled with images of me, maybe to be brought out again as memories, fodder for fantasies.

Fuck. So erotic.

Jacob urged me to lie down, and as the cool of the leather seeped into my shoulder blades, he hoisted my legs up into the stirrups, spreading my pussy wide open, putting it in full view of the audience. I tried to remember who had been behind the windows that would have the best vantage point. Was it the woman with the up-do or another middle-aged man I'd spotted—a man who'd licked his lips as I'd walked past?

I couldn't remember.

It. Didn't. Matter.

Jacob was between my legs. I glanced down and saw him releasing his cock. Huge and swollen, it jutted from his new leather trousers, his abdomen tense, the neat row of muscles coated in a sheen of sweat.

Arching my back, I shifted on the bench, tried to angle my hips to him, but it was impossible. My legs, high and secured in the stirrups, rendered me his prisoner.

"You look so damn wanton, like a porn star or something," he said, shoving his trousers down further, then stepping out of them.

There was a moment of shuffling and I guessed he was removing his shoes and socks.

"You look like you were made for sex, made for me, your dripping pussy, your big tits and your hot, tight arse. I'm going to fuck you so hard, so good in front of all these people. They all know what you want, whore. They know you're a dirty little slut and you can take it, all of it, from me."

Listening to him talk, revelling in his filthy words, Jacob caught me unawares when he plunged his fingers into my pussy.

The muscles in my back contracted and my neck bowed. He'd filled me quickly and roughly, was treating my body as though it was for his enjoyment, his penetration. I tossed my arms up and over my head, my shoulders stretching as he twisted and turned his fingers inside me. His knuckles scraped on my butt cheeks as he forged in, jabbing my cervix, pounding my G-spot. It was brutally horny, deliciously submissive.

His thumb scraped over my clit, and again I groaned behind the ball. I felt lightheaded and turned to my left. It took me a second to focus on a man and woman staring at me. I hadn't noticed them before. He was sharply suited; she wore a sequined top and sat on his lap, her bush of red hair almost obscuring his view of me being hand fucked. I stared into his eyes as my body was jostled industriously, feeling the glorious first tug of an orgasm building. My tongue curled, as did my toes. Jacob was going to give it to me with his hand.

Suddenly, he pulled out. I whimpered in frustration, but then his cock was there and with one almighty thrust he surged in, banging the air from my lungs and moving my body up the bench. I turned back to him. His mouth was stretched in a feral grimace as he plundered in and out. My breasts jigged wildly, the clamps tugging and pulling as gravity added to their torment.

I was coming, it was there. Trying to shout, I released muffled grunts and wails that echoed, along with the slap of flesh on flesh, around the room. I felt almost mad with excitement at what was happening. Everyone's eyes were on me. Fixated on my pleasure.

"Ah, yes, come, come…" Jacob shouted, slamming into me harder than ever before.

Every nerve in my body tingled then surged as my orgasm

claimed me with a ferocity that bordered on violent. I twisted and writhed, no longer in control of my own being, pleasure my only sensation as my pussy clung to and released Jacob's dick over and over. I closed my eyes as I swooped in and out of reality. That had been one incredible fuck, one seriously intense orgasm.

Jacob's cock slowed and then, as my breathing settled, he pulled out.

He hadn't come. His cock gleamed with my moisture, the head beet-red and swollen. I looked into his face but couldn't make out his expression as he began to unstrap my legs.

Glancing at the windows, I noticed the first suited man I'd seen was masturbating. His hand had disappeared, but the tell-tale movements of his shoulder and his flared nostrils and set jaw gave the game away.

A thrill went through me. He'd obviously enjoyed the show so far.

Good.

My legs were both down. My hips complained, but I ignored them.

"On your hands and knees," Jacob ordered. Then, clearly not feeling patient, he lifted and turned me over on the bench.

My palms sank into the soft leather, and I shifted my knees so they were right underneath me, ensuring my on-all-fours position was nice and symmetrical. I wanted to think about the details – there were lots of eyes casting their scrutiny over our performance. A performance, it seemed, that would now include Jacob fucking me from behind.

Or so I thought.

As my heart still pounded from the ferocity of my climax and I fought for air through my nose, a slippery, lubed finger delved into my anus. I jolted upwards in surprise, but Jacob quickly placed a firm hand on the small of my back.

"Relax," he said hoarsely.

He worked the lubrication around my tight hole in deep, penetrating circles, greasing me up thoroughly inside and out.

I dropped my head and groaned. Once again, when not expecting anal play, Jacob was giving it to me. Once again I adored the depraved sensation. Performing such a base, primitive act in front of our audience made it seedier, all the more scandalous.

They could all see how much I adored my rear hole being breached. There was no hiding the clawing of my fingers on the side of the bench, the ecstatic fluttering of my eyes.

Two fingers worked my passage now, demanding more give.

"Ah, yes, open up, like that," Jacob murmured, stretching me wide. "So pretty, so pink, so soft, so ready now."

He slipped his fingers from me, and my thighs and spine braced for the invasion, though I kept my arsehole loose and pliant—*Oh, God, that fucking word turns me on*—waiting for his dick to widen my sphincter. I was hardly able to contain my excitement, and had I not been gagged I would have been shouting for it.

But what I felt against my hole wasn't the smooth head of his cock. It was cool and domed and unyieldingly hard.

My mind fuzzed; I gasped. It was the end of the flogger we'd brought with us from the hotel room. The one I'd used as a dildo the afternoon before.

I squirmed, and his hands, coated in my juice and lube, slid around my stomach and gripped me, holding me up and exactly where he wanted me.

"Take it," he said. "It's what your audience wants to see. You with your arse stuffed full, a big, thick handle penetrating your slutty hole, and they know you're going to love it. It's going to make you want to come all over again. Take it, whore, take it."

His horny words washed over me, and I tried to relax more, allow the handle to penetrate me. I dripped with lube, my arsehole pre-stretched.

"Good girl, just let me do it."

He increased the pressure and the dome popped into me, wide and cool. It stung like crazy, creating a dark, twisted pleasure in my gut. I groaned loud and abandoned, the deep rumble in my chest vibrating through my teeth and jostling the ball in my mouth.

"Yes, that's it," he murmured. "Now take a few inches."

I shut my eyes, riding on sensations that tingled from my poor abused nipples to my recently stimulated clit and onto my buggered portal. My unruly body clenched around the rod, disobeying my will to relax, but the clasping sensation just heightened my arousal, fed yet more stimulation to my clit and pussy.

"Yes, that's it, that's enough," Jacob said as he released me. "Now arch your back."

I hung my head and groaned again.

"Do it," he said more firmly. "Arch your back and hold your head high. Look around at the people staring at you."

His body heat left me.

"This is what you wanted, Karen. This is what's in your filthy book. A shocking, lewd show for strangers. Allowing people to see you at your most primitive, receiving pleasure you can barely even admit to thinking about, let alone taking, let alone allowing spectators to watch."

I opened my eyes. The gothic young couple were kissing. He had one eye on me, his hands inside the girl's top. I imagined their excitement and it upped my own. Next to them a suited man had his palm flat on the window and his nose pressed against the glass. Further along the row yet another man appeared to be wanking, and a woman with tatty blonde hair chewed gum as she stared at me.

Next to her was the club's receptionist.

"You know what they're thinking, don't you?" Jacob said in his best 'rapist' voice. "They think that not only are you a filthy, horny bitch, but that you also look like a horse. You've got a bit in your mouth so I can control you and a great big tail coming out of your arse. Oh, if only you could see your slutty self. Your breasts swinging and heavy with the metal clamps and the fronds of the flogger touching your thighs."

I didn't need a mirror to imagine the shocking sight I was at that moment in my life.

"Twitch your tail," Jacob said. "Go on, shake your tail."

Trying to be obedient, I jerked my hips and the soft strands of the flogger swept over my clammy thighs. The heavy handle shifted inside me, and I groaned at the illicit sensation.

"More."

I repeated the action, the penetration deepening with each movement. I was so invaded, so possessed – stuffed almost to bursting point.

"Yes, that's it. In fact, you deserve a treat for that little show." He came to the head end of the table. "Drop down to your elbows."

I did as he asked, and my face came level with his bobbing cock.

He fiddled at the back of my head, and the ball slid from my mouth.

"I need your mouth free for this next bit," he said, dropping the gag to the floor. "Oh, no, keep your mouth open." He squeezed his hands on my cheeks and forced my jaw to stay wide. "Here, take me, all of me."

He tugged at his shaft and offered forward his shiny, eager cockhead.

I salivated and would have licked my lips if I could.

He rode in, not fast and furious, just so the domed underside of his glans sat past my teeth.

"Oh, yes, fuck, look at everyone watching, watching me sinking into your mouth. Your mouth, your arse, your pussy, it all belongs to me. Brace for it, slut, I'm going to give you every bit of my big, hard cock."

I lapped at the cream in his slit and pulled his taste onto my tongue. The flavour of my cunt was mixed with his musky rawness. Since he'd paused, I flicked at his frenulum, knowing it drove him crazy, gliding around the tiny, taut band of skin and tapping it sideways in small zigzag movements.

"Ah, Jesus, that feels good. And fuck, what a horny bitch you are with your tail in the air and your lips around my dick." With that, he sank deep, plunging his salty thickness to the very back of my throat.

I battled to take all of him, fighting my gag reflex.

"Ahhh, yes, yes," Jacob hissed, catching hold of my head in his palms. "Yes, take it, take me, you can do it." His voice was tremor-filled, lust-infused, and judging by the steeliness of his shaft, he was close to the edge.

Setting up a quick, steady rhythm by bobbing up and down, I used all my best oral skills—tightening my lips, sucking hard and gulping his glans down my throat when he reached maximum penetration.

"Oh, fuck, I'm too close." He pulled out. His cock looked angry, and he fisted it and stepped away.

"Jacob," I gasped, reaching forwards for him.

"Keep still."

His long, naked body disappeared from my view. Then he was behind me again, pulling me to the end of the bench and lowering my feet to the floor. The flogger was still in my arse. The handle moved and rolled as my position changed, causing me to gasp and clench it.

"Look at the windows," he said. "Look at your audience. They want to know you're aware of their presence. Look, Karen, look. Show them you care."

I raised my head, stared around at the faces. Some were tense and wide-eyed, others relaxed but interested. I settled my concentration on the receptionist, looked into her face and wondered if she was wishing she were in my position with Jacob doing all of this stuff to her.

I'd bet my damn filthy book she was.

"Ahh, ahh," I cried, screwing up my eyes and rising to my tiptoes.

Jacob was moving the handle inside me.

"Shh," he said. He pulled the flogger out, and there was a thump as it fell to the floor.

Part of me was relieved. Part of me missed it so much I wanted to cry.

"I've shown everyone that I like to fuck your cunt and your mouth, now it's time for me to fuck your arse, whore, so get ready for it."

There was no further preamble. His cock was at my anus, nudging forwards, gaining purchase. I gripped the side of the bench and twisted my head to look at the windows on my right. The girl chewing gum had frozen with her mouth wide. Had she ever been fucked up the arse? Judging by her rapt expression, I guessed not.

Suddenly Jacob pistoned in. He made no allowance for my small, tight hole and rammed his dick to the hilt. His balls slapped hard against my vulva and I cried out, adoring the sudden, brutal filling.

"Ah, fuck yes." He gripped my hips, held me tight and firm and pounded in and out. A few times he withdrew completely then blasted back in, stretching my scorched anus anew with his wide glans.

I felt helpless, like a rag doll with orifices for his use. My arse was on fire, my pussy weeping, and my nipples dragged painfully on the bench as he jostled into me. Every sensation was erotic and torturous.

Bliss wrapped in depravity.

"Ah, yes, come. Come, whore," he ordered.

I couldn't see his face but I could imagine his head tipped back to the ceiling, the tendons on his neck straining, his teeth bared.

I shot my hand down to my clit. "Oh, yes, yes, harder, fuck me harder," I wailed, not caring that I had surrendered to screaming my needs. It only took three nudges on my hard, swollen nub and I climaxed. I was so close anyway. "Fuck me, fuck me, fuck me," I shouted, reeling over wave after satisfying wave of delight. "Fuckmefuckmefuckme."

He obliged, and as I pulsed and spasmed on the bench, he

flooded my arse with his pleasure, a long, hot shot of cum that warmed my insides and soaked his cock.

"Oh, God, yes," he shouted, stilling as deep as he could go. "Ah, yes."

I released my hypersensitive clit and gripped the bench again. Allowed my orgasm to ravage through my pussy and rectum and squeezed every drop of pleasure from every nerve possible.

Jacob gave one final shunt into me then his body was over mine, his chest touching my shoulder blades and the mask rubbing against my hair. His breaths were a raging storm in my ear.

A whirring sound scraped around the room.

Panting, I opened my eyes and noticed the automatic curtains closing. The last face I saw was the man who'd definitely been wanking.

Chapter Thirteen

Life had got back to normal so quickly once we'd arrived home that it was almost like Amsterdam had never happened. A dream of my making – a damn wonderful dream that I pulled out at my leisure, reliving time and again while alone. Sometimes even when Jacob fucked me. The memories gave my orgasms a sharper bite, and I had to will myself not to cry out too loudly and wake the girls.

My orgasms had intensified during this journey of rediscovery and so had our relationship. There was nothing dreary about our lives together. I'm sure to the outside world we were just like any other married couple in our cul-de-sac, me a little tubby and not terribly fashionable, Jacob often unshaven and overtired because of work demands. But I knew different. *We* knew different. Because sure, the effort of running a home and bringing up two energetic little girls could be exhausting, emotionally and physically, but we still found time for one another – whispered desires at the kitchen sink, a naughty text when I knew he was in a meeting, or a sexy rendezvous in any room in the house if the girls were on simultaneous play dates.

One of the most delicious new additions to my life was the sizzle of anticipation and the sexual tension that could come from a day of thinking about what we had planned once the girls were asleep. Jacob was always willing, never disappointed me and always made me feel like his most precious, adored possession, even when his coarse whispers were sinfully filthy.

One night, as we were getting ready for bed, he'd given my rump a slap and called me a slut in his best bad-boy voice. My whole body had hummed with delight until I heard the toilet flush and realised one of the girls was up.

We both froze, caught one another's gaze and waited to see if one of our daughters would appear at the bedroom door.

They didn't.

Thank goodness.

We'd entertained the thought of soundproofing our room on more than one occasion, dismissing it as a frivolous expense, but Jacob had got a bonus from securing a big deal and as the girls grew older, our dilemma would increase.

Hence the two workmen in our bedroom now; nailing, banging, fixing.

They would be done soon, and no one would be any the wiser. A new stud wall would be placed over the soundproofing materials, a special door fitted to match the other rooms, and as far as anyone else was concerned, we'd just redecorated. Tomorrow I planned to sit sewing while the painters did their bit in there and they painted the spare room too. The fresh coat we'd neglected to paint when Jacob had…

God, since that first time we'd indulged in anal play and bondage so often, like kids with a new toy. It was still novel enough not to become boring, but I worried if we did it too often it could. We needed to mix it up, find new ways of creating pleasure, or switch things around so we never did the same thing twice in a row.

That filthy book came to mind then, and I left the kitchen, not caring that these men were in our home and that I was meant to be making them coffee with two bloody sugars and 'just a splash of milk, pet'. I rushed upstairs, standing on tiptoe to push the attic door that would release the lock and let it swing down. Reaching up, I grabbed hold of the metal ladder jutting halfway across the square opening and dragged it down. It clattered loudly, the two sections clicking into place as the base met the landing.

"Coffee won't be a minute!" I called, gingerly climbing

the ladder.

My stomach bunched at the fact I was actually going up into the roof, something I always left to Jacob. I was all right getting up there, sort of—the banister being beside the ladder and me worrying I'd pitch over it and tumble down the stairs didn't help—it was getting down that would prove a problem. But I'd do it because I wanted to get hold of that book again. There were so many fantasies in there, ones every couple tried and others they most certainly did not. But if I remembered correctly, there was one in particular that Jacob had already mentioned and it had gripped me lately. Imagining it in my mind before I fell asleep had created dreams that tortured me with their sexual intensity. They'd been so vivid I would have sworn I'd actually been fucked, my cunt sopping, the sheets beneath me damp from my juices, my hand firmly between my legs, leaving me in no doubt I'd fondled myself while I slept.

The ladder creaked ominously as I climbed inside. With my heart pounding erratically, I crawled across the plywood covering the fluffy yellow insulation, unable to bring myself into a hunched-over crouch. Hands and knees would have to do. It was dark until I reached up and tugged the cord that switched on the light. The bare bulb emitted too bright a light and I squinted at an attic full on all sides, although Jacob had packed things in an orderly way. Two bed frames rested against the far wall, as did the dining table and chairs we'd had too many years ago to count, in its pre-erected state, a regimented row of legs, chair backs and seats, the worn tabletop behind them. To my left sat the pink plastic baby bath I'd used for the girls, and a potty I'd kept just in case we'd decided on having more children. We hadn't, agreeing two was enough for us, and I thought about doing a car boot sale to get rid of them. There was a lot of stuff up here that was junk to us but treasure to someone else, and the money we would generate could be put to good use by purchasing new toys for us. Adult toys.

I looked over at the space opposite, trying not to think how many spiders and creepy crawlies lurked in the crevices. I glanced up, seeing the inevitable webs, thick and weighted down by dust. I returned my attention to what was in front of me, suppressing a shudder.

Containers of all sizes, with black marker pen proclaiming boldly what they held inside, appeared as a higgledy-piggledy beige wall. I scanned them, noting that some housed old clothes, blankets, and crockery. Others were filled with magazines from when we'd needed ideas on how to do up the house, and others still contained knick-knacks I couldn't bear to part with, even though I would never have them on the shelves again. But one red box sat there, in the top right-hand corner, with no black marker wording, its only decoration a few overlapping strips of brown sticky tape and the original logo from when the box had been the home for packs of frozen spare ribs.

My box.

My book.

I gasped, smiling so hard it hurt. Giddy with excitement, I scrabbled over to the boxes and reached up to pull mine down. Nostalgia hit, a great wave of the past covering me from head to foot in goosebumps. I recalled packing my things so vividly it was like I'd done it yesterday. I smelt my old bedroom, recalled the state of it, junk all around as I'd taped the box closed. My feelings from that time returned then, full force and blunt—shame, embarrassment, guilt, a vow never to read the book again. But here I was, fingers itching to rip back that brown tape, toss every other book aside and clutch that filthy book to my chest.

The ripping of the tape sounded obscenely loud, and I glanced over my shoulder at the insane thought that the workmen might have heard it. So what if they had? Why was I even bothered? Funny how strange things entered the mind like that. Did some of the old guilt still linger, was that it? Would it always be ingrained in me, a patch of mould that could grow and grow until it infested me once again?

I wouldn't allow it.

This time was different. *This* time I could embrace what the book said, do every damn thing it suggested, providing Jacob was game.

And I had no doubt he would be.

I peeled back the four top flaps, taking the time to run my fingertips along the spines so the lids didn't spring closed again. The scent of cardboard, musty from years of being in an attic, wafted up to greet me. And that special smell, of ageing books, all semi-damp dust and yellowing pages, made me think of university days in the library, dissertations being written with the deadline looming. Feet shuffling on the cheap, flat-pile brown carpet. Shelves stacked high, books sticking out, some lopsided and others bolt upright.

I knew where the guilt had come from, then. It wasn't what the book contained, not really, but that I'd checked it out of the library without taking it back. The librarian had given me such a look of disdain as she'd slammed the date stamper down on the form inside the front cover that I hadn't wanted to return it—to be given the same look again. She'd made me feel, when I read the book, that it had been wrong. That the events inside had been wrong. Maybe even immoral. But they weren't, I knew that now, not when they were performed by two consenting adults.

Absurdly, I wanted to cry. That woman had planted a kernel of doubt in my mind at a tender age, and it had sprouted, stayed with me for years, even though I'd talked dirty to Jacob right at the start, before the girls had come along. Even then I'd worried a little that what came out of my mouth made me a filthy person, that I was all kinds of corrupt. Yet I'd still said them. Still enjoyed the result of them. Then becoming a mother had stripped everything away, as though enjoying sex as much as I could wasn't an option anymore. And my obsession with making sure the books we checked out of the library these days were returned promptly made sense now. I didn't mind taking *those* books back. Children's adventures and good, clean romance fiction. I could saunter in there, head held high, knowing the librarian wouldn't even look up at me as she scanned the barcodes inside the books and nodded that, yes, I could select some new ones now.

Hell, I might even borrow a dirty book again; see how it felt now I was more adult and didn't give a damn what anyone thought.

Thank God I'd woken up. And thank God Jacob had joined me on this new journey.

I removed the books one by one, placing them gently on the plywood, stalling the moment when I'd see that filthy book again. Although I'd seen another copy in Amsterdam, it wasn't the same. This was *my* book—even though it technically still belonged to the library—and it was in English. It had page corners folded over, I remembered that now, and a splash of Coke coated one page where I'd spurted it from my mouth in shock at what I'd read.

Would those same words shock me now?

I didn't think so.

There was one book left to remove before I'd see my prize. I lifted it, deliberately not looking inside the box, and popped it onto the pile with the others. They slewed sideways, much like the ones in Amsterdam, and I stared at the domino effect, a fan of well-loved literature. *To Kill a Mockingbird, A Clockwork Orange, Macbeth* and *Hamlet*. A few cheesy romances that brought a smile. A couple of detective thrillers from when I'd fancied myself the kind of girl who could work out who the killer was, then realised I hadn't when it came to the reveal. A glut of memories, all attached to those pages. Clothes I'd worn, hairstyles I'd sported, food I'd eaten, people I'd hung around with… God, it had all gone by so fast.

I turned to look at the wall opposite, delaying the final moment some more, enjoying the recall of my youth. And then I'd met Jacob, tousle-haired Jacob who had turned my world upside down and still kept turning it. The man who had cared for me without question since that first day and continued to do so.

Tears pricked my eyes, the reminiscence too much, and I took a deep breath before plunging one hand inside that spare rib box and taking hold of the book. I took it out, settled the bottom of it on my folded legs and stared down at it. *My Erotic Fantasies* sung from the front cover, although it had dulled with time, the previously bright red font more burgundy now. And the entwined naked couple, they didn't look as lurid as they had back in the day, similar to any number of books out there now that didn't make anyone bat an eyelid.

The long and short of it was that time had changed things. This book didn't really need to be hidden anymore, would no longer be considered base by most people, could sit on my bookshelf without anyone thinking anything of it—except maybe to raise an eyebrow and look at us in a slightly different light, but I would still keep it under wraps in case our girls decided on a nosing spree and discovered it.

I ran my fingertips over it, then thumbed the pages before telling myself to just get on with it and open the damn thing. I did, and my cunt flooded at the sight of those lewd words. I sat for some time, scouring the pages, imagining the positions and scenarios in my head, but a sharp set of hammer raps from below brought me back to the present.

"Shit, their coffee!"

I gathered the fallen books together and put them back in the box, securing it as best I could with tape that didn't fancy being sticky anymore. Hefting it back onto the wall, I scooped that filthy book from the floor and shuffled over to the attic opening. Peering down, I bit my lip. The landing seemed miles away, and my stomach rolled as I contemplated how I would turn at the hatch and get down the ladder. Book still in hand, I scooted around, legs trembling, and felt with one foot for a rung. My leg dangled in mid-air, meeting nothing, and panic set in. I *had* to get back down, and I could do it, too, if I pulled up my new, lacy, big-girl panties and told myself to stop being such a fool.

I found a rung, relief warming my insides, and somehow managed to make my wobbly way down the ladder with the book still in hand. Feeling happier once I was stood on the landing, I popped the ladder catches and shoved it back into the attic. The hatch proved harder to close, the bloody thing not playing the game and refusing to lock. I let out a strangled sound of annoyance and tried one more time, grunting with satisfaction as the door stayed shut. Hot and sweaty, I spun to rush downstairs and make the damn coffee, only to run smack into a broad, white T-shirted chest that gave off the scent of hard work.

I looked up, whipping the book behind my back and stared at one of the workmen. "Sorry. I'm just off to make your coffee now." *After scanning through the filthiest book I've ever read and wanting my husband to come home for lunch so he can fuck me ragged when you and your friend are gone.*

"No, my fault," he said, stepping back with his hands raised. "I didn't expect you to turn round so fast." He laughed, the kind that showed he felt uncomfortable, that by him touching me he thought he'd maybe overstepped the mark. "Um, we've finished plastering now. It'll be ready to paint tomorrow like we promised."

I studied him quickly, noting his flushed cheeks, plaster-spattered brown hair, hazel eyes that darted warily from side to side as if he expected Jacob to come tearing along any second and punch his lights out. I felt sorry for him—it had been entirely my fault—and I shook my head, laughing.

"No, no. My fault. I got distracted up there." I pointed to the hatch with my free hand, and the book slid within my grip. *Please, do* not *let me drop it.* "I'll just go and get your coffee on now."

"Yep. Thanks. We're ready for that, all this hard work."

He smiled, but not the lecherous kind that would've told me he knew damn well why we'd had our room soundproofed. I wondered if my excuse of using it as a bedroom-stroke-music studio had been believed.

"Right. Okay. Two coffees, both with two sugars and a splash of milk coming right up."

I nipped past him and hared down the stairs, the book by my side closest to the wall so he couldn't see what I was holding. As I rounded the bottom newel post and swung myself around in the direction of the kitchen, I imagined that if he saw the book and thought of the soundproofing, he'd think me and Jacob were a raging pair of pervs.

Did I care?

The wonderful feeling sweeping through me told me that, no, I didn't bloody well care, and brought on a surge of laughter. Once in the kitchen, I let it free, leaning over onto the counter until tears ran and my stomach muscles ached. God, it was so good to feel this way—seeing then reading the book again hadn't made me feel tainted and wrong.

I was finally me, Karen, a liberated woman, no shackles with regards to my sex life. With the room complete and a door lock in place, we wouldn't have to go away for time alone. It was getting old having people wink at us when we told them we were off, nudging our ribs and saying 'dirty weekend' far too often and with sickening glee. We wouldn't have to have people *knowing* we were having sex, didn't have to explain why we needed time alone—we could just do it, no explanations. Yes, our bedroom revamp had cost a pretty penny, but the money we'd save on hotel rooms would make up for it eventually.

And why was I even trying to justify it anyway? It was our life, our money to do with as we pleased.

I stood upright, wiped my eyes and sniffed. Re-boiled the kettle and went about making instant coffee. The workmen came down, thanked me as I handed over their cups, and went out into the garden to drink. I stared at them through the window. Bright sunlight shone on their hair, and they rocked on the balls of their feet, scrubbed their chins, and probably discussed their next job. I wondered if they'd tell their wives about the couple who'd had their bedroom soundproofed because they wanted to try their hand at singing. The workman's wife, she'd know that was a lie, and maybe it would make her think. I hoped it would, if she was even told about our soundproof bedroom. Perhaps it would help them revitalise their relationship. If they ended up feeling like we did, it could only be a good thing, couldn't it?

* * * *

Another evening, another round of bedtime rituals. Baths, stories, little girls tucked beneath quilts. I took a quick shower, knowing that by the time I emerged, Tess and Lucy would be fast asleep. They'd been on a school trip today, to a working farm where they'd got to feed the animals and help muck out the pigs. They'd stunk to high heaven when they'd returned home, their boots relegated to the patio so they didn't fill the house with their stench. I'd give them a good scrub tomorrow, but for now I wanted to spend time with Jacob and try out our new bedroom.

As I dried myself, I thought about how lovely it was going to be, screaming if I wanted to or letting the bed creak; the headboard smack against the wall. The fear of being heard would be a distant memory, and we could love one another as we'd been doing lately, in the comfort of our own bed.

Or on the floor. Against the wall...

I slipped on my black négligée, the one Jacob liked to watch me wearing. With a spritz of perfume in all the right places, I made my way downstairs, stopping in the living room doorway and striking a seductive pose. Jacob sat on the sofa, thumbing the remote, and took his gaze from the TV immediately.

"Ah, you're on a mission, I see." He smiled, dropping the remote beside him, and beckoning for me to join him. "Come here."

I walked across the room towards him, feeling all kinds of sexy and adored, and knelt on the floor to pull out that filthy book from beneath the sofa where I'd placed it after the workmen had left. I sat beside him, flung one leg over his, and snuggled close.

"You still want to read this with me?" I asked, glancing up to look at his face.

He eyed the cover for a second then met my eyes, and there was that glint there, sparkling and full of promise. "Yep."

"There's one thing in here that I think you will like particularly. I read it in the attic earlier, but didn't get to the part I wanted."

"Oh, right. Get on with it then."

I fluttered through the pages, struggling to remember where the fantasy I wanted to show Jacob was, but eventually stopped the flow of paper around the three-quarter mark. One corner had been dutifully turned down at chapter eleven. I held the book between us and we both read, me impatient to turn to the next page because I read faster than him.

And there it was, three pages in, one of the things we had yet to try. It was about something Jacob had done before he'd met me—watching porn. Except this fantasy... God, *this* fantasy encouraged the couple to act out the porn they watched. Move for move. Stroke for stroke. Thrust for thrust.

I looked at him again, into eyes that sparkled brightly. His cheeks had flushed from what he was reading and his cock, beneath his jeans, nudged my wrist—his hard and wanting cock.

"You fancy trying this?" I asked casually, knowing he would, needing a quick answer because I couldn't wait to get up there into our room. "With our DVD from Amsterdam or the new movie I bought over the internet the other day?"

"A *new* movie? Jesus, Karen, you just keep on surprising me." He eyed me, head tilting. "You watched it already?"

"No. I thought we could watch it together. Do what this book says. I read the back of the DVD, and it's about some guy who uses a hammer to… We never did get to use the handle of the one we bought when we stayed in the hotel that time."

He let out a stuttered breath, raised his hand to caress my cheek. "Christ, I love you."

"I know." I grinned and lifted my hand to cover his. "So, you want this fantasy? The porn?"

"Fuck, yes, but more than that. I want…you, always."

Thief

Excerpt

Prologue

The jeweller stretched thick arms above his head, linked sturdy fingers and rotated his calloused palms towards the ceiling. As the stretch travelled down his aching spine, a tap on the office door accompanied by a sharp trill jerked his head to the right.

"John, Miss Worthington-Hurley is here to collect her ring." A pause then another rap. "John, John, can you hear me?"

"Yep, be right there," he called in a rough voice as he lowered his arms and pushed to his feet. A nerve in his jaw twitched as he forced weight onto his left leg. "Dead son of a bitch," he muttered.

Using the table for support he moved to the safe and pulled out Miss Worthington-Hurley's ring. He slipped it into a black velvet box embossed with gold lettering, flicked open the lock on his door and limped to the front of the shop. As he stepped into the glittering display area, he pasted a dazzling smile on his rugged features and forced a flame to life in his eyes. "Miss Worthington-Hurley, such a pleasure to see you," he said brightly.

"Mr. Taylor." The young woman bounced to the glass counter, blonde bob swishing, blue eyes flashing. "I trust you are well."

"Fine, thank you, and yourself?"

"Fine, great… excited actually… really, really excited." She clasped her hands beneath her chin and skipped on the spot.

"I thought you'd be looking forward to finally getting it." He held the small black box over the counter. "The alteration went fine. No hitches. I think you'll find the fit perfect."

She flicked open the lid and sucked air through glossed lips. "Oh… I'd forgotten how beautiful it is. It's completely stunning… Don't you think?"

"It is indeed, flawless in every way. You could not have chosen better, madam."

She pulled the ring from the spongy holding and slid it onto her left ring finger. "It fits perfectly. You're so clever. It feels made especially for me."

"It was made especially for you."

She held the three-stoned ring up to the artificial lights, tilted her hand and sighed as the light fracturing through pebbled the counter with frantic stars. "Thank you so much. You've done a simply marvellous job."

"My pleasure."

"Has Tobias settled the account?" she asked, scooping the presentation box into a Gucci handbag.

"He has, and once again, congratulations on your engagement." John leant his hip against the counter and shifted his weight.

"Thank you, you're so kind. We'll be in to sort out the wedding rings when we've set a date."

"Very good."

She pulled her handbag onto her shoulder, tapped across the redwood floor and breezed onto Park Lane, leaving behind a cloud of spiced perfume.

John's smile slipped as he left the display area. There were no other customers in the shop. Just two junior female assistants chatting quietly as they conducted a laborious stock take.

He secured the lock on his office door, reached into a metal filing cabinet and withdrew a half full bottle of whisky. He splashed a triple into a stained mug and downed two-thirds in two gulps. He sank into his chair, shoved up his sleeves and pushed a heavy microscope to one side. The solid steel base scattered several delicate instruments onto the floor. He left them lying haphazardly—a complicated game of pick-up sticks.

He crossed corded forearms on the table and rested his head on a deeply ingrained snake tattoo. His eyes shut, his mind drifted. Alcohol eased the way.

Suddenly, he was hit with the stale scent of unwashed men and the creaking sound of straining canvas overhead. The atmosphere was studied, the tension mounting. He could hear himself asking questions, making calculated, important decisions, yet like being on a plane and waiting for ears to pop, his own voice sounded unfamiliar and watery. He took a deep breath and watched the Al Jezzera broadcast. Was there anything he could glean? His mind whirred through the finer details of the intelligence, piecing it like a macabre jigsaw he knew off by heart.

He raised his head, disorientated, and squinted into the staring glare of a table lamp. Remembered where he was, in his office. He reached clumsily for his mug, swallowed, banged it down and fumbled for the light switch. His eyes closed once more, and sleep claimed him.

The temperature plummeted. He was being jolted over stones and boulders. His jaw rattled and his spine tensed. The wheel suspension groaned its complaint. He studied Cobra One. They were an intimidating bunch. From their boots to their balaclavas, everything was the colour of the darkest night, including exposed flesh. Gadgetry and hardware bulged from every pocket, their outfits swollen with deadly loads. There was an atmosphere of grim anticipation. An energised but sombre tension only men going into battle emit, it filled the APV, inhabiting the space like another physical presence.

He jumped onto a ruined suburban road. Dust scattered around his heavy boots as his legs absorbed the impact. His night vision goggles gave the area a surreal green glow. A skinny Afghan dog stopped and stared, luminous pupils flashing, then it ran away, whip tail straight as a cane.

He was outside the house now—dilapidated, barely a roof and only three and a half walls. No complete windows and rusting corrugated iron wedged as a feeble fence. He flattened against the pock-marked wall at the north side with Eagle and Hig. The other three men rounded the corner to the south side to act as deadly lookouts.

Through the shadows, he saw his own gloved hand sign three, two, one. The door frame brushed his shoulder as he ducked through the narrow gap. He came face to face with a bearded man—stained turban, round glasses, the right lens cracked like a lightening fork—with a primed AK47 in his hand.

John's reflex created a sickening crack. He felt the soft flesh of broken neck on his forearm and the slack of dead tendons melt over his wrist. He lowered the body to the floor.

He tuned into the low hum of distant conversation. Hig and Eagle moved in tight behind him, and although he couldn't hear them, he knew they were following. Adrenaline raced through his veins, his heart rate sped. His senses were sharp, acute, alive.

The voices were clearer now, men laughing and talking in Arabic, high pitched and jabbering. He reached the end of the passageway and came to a splintered door, which was open a convenient crack. He flicked his head and eyeballed the candle-lit room to see what they were dealing with. Two hostages, bound and gagged, sat in the far left corner, five armed insurgents hung around, weapons relaxed.

He braced for the contact, gathered his energy, ready to burst into the room. His nerves were on fire, his survival instincts in control.

Suddenly gun shots burst from the street outside. Ear splitting cracks. His men out the front had been spotted.

His forward momentum switched to a hasty retreat down the corridor with Eagle and Hig.

Treacherous light filled the passageway as the door was flung open. Frantic Arabic shouts punctuated the air, and John knew their shadowy figures had been seen.

Eagle and Hig ducked out into the night. But spinning just past the dead guard, John was greeted with the unblinking eye of a gun. He raised his weapon and fired a double tap, watched two small black holes appear on a surprised forehead. They oozed as the body crumpled.

He ducked outside and slammed his back against the wall. "Shit. We gotta get the hostages out now," he hissed.

Eagle swung his arm and rolled a flash bang into the house. It rattled like a tin can before exploding into a burst of lightening and slamming out a clap of thunder.

He charged back in, saw hazy, glowing movements in the swirling smoke and fired. The ground absorbed a solid thud. Hig's mass moved with him. More hysterical shouts and screams, terrified English accents mixed in with panicked Arabic.

"*Hostages down on the floor*!" The shouted words tore at the flesh of his throat. The sole of his boot connected with the door. He lined a standing man in his sights and pulled the trigger, twice. Hig and Eagle flanked him, mimicked him. Three satisfyingly heavy thumps.

Five down.

Mission complete.

Four more thunderous shots rang out. Chest…violence… no air. A force like a charging bull flung him on top of the terrified hostages. Pain in his back circled and squeezed his body armour, pushing every scrap of air from his lungs. He gasped for breath like a fish out of water, suffocating on empty lung cavities. There was a shocking tearing sensation in his left leg. The agony was sickening, every nerve in his body screamed for attention. He caught his breath, cried out—a primitive, guttural scream. He dropped his gun, grabbed for his leg, sure it would be gone, sure he would feel nothing but a soggy stump. His mind was a white blank of panic. Death smiled at him.

"Shit, boss there were six of them." Eagle swung his gun away from a now slumped body in a concealed nook behind the door.

Hig bent double, taut blue tourniquet in his hand. There was sorrow in his eyes, a look of sympathy, and in that unguarded second, before professionalism intercepted, John knew it was all over for him…

Another bang on the office door brought him home from his secret duties.

"We're off now, John, its five-thirty."

"Okay." His voice was hoarse. He reached for the last drop of whisky. "I'll be right out to lock up." He flicked on the light, pushed up and headed out the office with only a hint of a limp. At the front door, he said a final goodbye to his colleagues. They didn't know it was the last goodbye, but he did.

He performed the elaborate locking ritual for the last time and set the high tech alarm then pinched up the gems he'd been working on that morning—the three diamonds he'd expertly removed from Miss Worthington-Hurley's engagement ring and replaced with cheap cubic zirconia. He dropped them into a small, well-used fold in the lining of his trousers and smoothed down his shirt. After switching off the light he grabbed his jacket and headed into the early evening sunshine humming an old tune. Life was finally on the up. Soon, he'd be readdressing the balance, equalling out all the shit inflicted on him since that fateful night.

Soon, he'd be living it up in the sun, away from endless physiotherapy, which caused nothing but more pain, away from London, away from all the reminders of what he used to have and of the man he used to be. It had taken a long time to squirrel away what the British tax payers owed him, what the British government had denied him, but now he had enough, enough to live in luxury for the foreseeable future and he couldn't wait to get on his way.

He walked slowly round the block to a secure car park, the pain in his knee nipping like piranhas now the whisky was beginning to wear off. For the millionth time, he wondered what those dumb ass do-gooders had been doing in Afghanistan. If they hadn't gone and got themselves taken hostage, he'd still have two functioning legs and a job he loved. He hated them. He knew it wasn't how a military man was supposed to think but he couldn't help it. They were as much to blame as the insurgents.

He shoved his hand into his pocket and pulled out a key fob. He clicked it once and a silver Porsche blinked to life, greeting him with a sharp, echoing beep.

Chapter One

Kat sat alone at the bar in The Fox and Goose. She felt weary, but that was plain old laziness. She'd hardly done anything all week, and last night's client, Kevin Milford, had been easy prey. He'd fallen instantly for her charms and almost as quickly into unconsciousness. He'd been pig ugly to look at all evening and more than a little dribbley to kiss, but at least, thank goodness, she hadn't had to have sex with him to take off with the goods. She was still thanking her lucky stars for that stroke of good fortune.

Tonight, once again, she'd spotted her hit soon after she'd entered the pub, partly because he looked exactly like he did on his photograph, but also because he was easily the biggest guy there, making him impossible to miss.

Brooding and alone, he sat hunched on his elbows nursing a tumbler of iced amber liquid. Kat took up a strategic position in his direct line of sight and, within minutes, trapped his gaze through the milling crowd.

His face was square and raw boned with hollows beneath jutting cheekbones, and he had a slightly hooked, but perfectly straight nose. She kept her gaze locked with his and let her thumb and index finger run up and slowly down the long, perilously thin stem of her glass of Sauvignon Blanc. It was a measured and deliberate gesture she knew would hold his attention and give him a clear idea of her intentions.

It did.

His wide mouth lifted and his pot-hole black eyes sparkled back across the bar with burning, dangerous intensity.

Kat let the corners of her glossed, scarlet lips rise in response, pulled her eyes away and went back to fake texting an imaginary friend. Tonight's hit was a distinct improvement in the appearance department. In fact, the two men couldn't have been more different. They were entirely different species from entirely different planets. Unlike Kevin's thin, weedy, asexual physique, John Taylor was a big, solid hunk of a man who looked as though he'd seriously overdosed on testosterone. His plain black T-shirt stretched over broad, powerful shoulders and a wide, defined chest. His biceps bulged beneath his skin and a snake tattoo coiled around his left forearm. Buzz cut, charcoal hair was cut in a neat, no-nonsense kind of way, yet he had considerably more than a five o'clock shadow spreading around his jaw and running down over his Adam's apple. Kat wondered why he'd been picked out for her to approach. He wasn't her usual type of client.

She looked back up to catch his eye and continue her

assault.

Her heart stuttered.

He was gone.

Shit, where was he?

She couldn't lose him. She scanned the other side of the bar.

He wasn't there either.

"May I?" A deep voice rumbled by her left shoulder. She spun and looked straight into the intense eyes she'd been searching for. Her heart rate didn't settle.

"Sure," she replied, trying to act nonchalant and forcing her body to appear relaxed.

He placed his drink on the bar, pulled up a vacant stool and sat his bulk down. "John," he said, holding out a colossal hand.

"Kat." Kat placed her hand in his and felt it completely enclosed in his warm palm. He held her firmly but gently, as if savouring the softness of her skin. She was used to this. It was how men usually held her, but John lingered even longer than most. She looked down at the grip, noticed the haze of dark hairs sweeping from his corded forearms, over his wide wrists and onto the back of his hand; a hand that could crush her bones in an instant without an iota of effort. For a second, she felt trapped, taken prisoner, but as soon as the feeling bubbled, he released her, reached for his drink and took a deep slug.

"Nice to meet you…Kat," he said after he'd mashed his lips together and swallowed. "Are you waiting for someone?"

"Well, I was." Kat wrinkled her nose. "But my friend just texted me to say she can't make it after all. She's having a family crisis, you know how it is." She spun her usual line, making it clear she was newly available for the whole evening.

"That's a shame." He didn't sound like he meant it in the slightest. "So, can I buy you another drink?" He indicated her nearly empty glass. "You know, try to salvage your evening since you're..." he cast his eyes downwards, a loitering, unselfconscious assessment of her whole body, "since you're done up all nice."

Kat rewarded his compliment with a dazzling smile and lifted her glass to her mouth. After she'd drained the last drip, she retrieved a spot of moisture from her lip with the tip of her tongue and said in a silky voice, "That would be very kind...John."

He cleared his throat and called to the barman, who he knew by name, ordered a double whisky and a large white wine. "Would you like to take a more comfortable seat?" He gestured to a corner sofa which had become free in the now busy pub.

Kat nodded and slid from the stool with her replenished drink. It was all going very well. Even if he was enormous, it made no difference. He'd be putty in her hands by the end of the evening. Once she'd played all her usual tricks, turned up the charm and let him fall under her spell.

She lifted her purse and led the way to ensure he got an optimum view of her curvy figure from behind. She arched the base of her spine, set down her shoulders and sashayed her hips. She sensed John's heated gaze burning through her tight black dress and heard him blow out a slow breath. She hoped he was imagining what it would be like to unzip her dress and roll off her stockings, slowly, one by one. He wouldn't get that far, but there was no harm in him thinking he would.

She sat, and he squeezed in close, his eyes glazed as if lost in a pool of dirty thoughts. Kat smiled and let her fingers drift to her new diamond necklace, let the moment stretch out in his mind by showing him how lovely she was to touch.

"So, Kat... I haven't seen you in here before." His attention was fixed considerably lower than her necklace.

"No, I haven't been in here before. But it's halfway between my friend's house and mine, so we thought it would be good for an evening of girly gossip."

"Gossip about what?"

"Oh, you know, this and that." Kat let go of the necklace and brushed long strands of her raven hair over her shoulders.

"This and that being the…er… men in your lives?"

Kat laughed, treating him to a flash of her perfect white teeth. "No, there are no men in either of our lives to gossip about." She tugged at the side of her bottom lip with her teeth, a gesture she hoped he'd find both erotic and innocent, and to let him know he had a very good chance of scoring, added, "Not at the moment anyway."

He grinned and leant his body closer as he lifted his drink. She knew he'd be getting a good hit of her delicate floral perfume because she was getting a nose full of his deeply masculine smell. It wasn't fancy, expensive aftershave. It was just soap and whisky and a whirl of raw pheromones, a full dose of the power of the opposite sex for any woman who got close enough to appreciate.

More books from Lily Harlem & Natalie Dae

Soul-aching desire was only the first layer of emotion around a secret I had to keep for all of time.

A dirty weekend in the country visiting sexy friends proves to be just the antidote.

Lori must prepare herself for the flogging of her life.

Pearl longs for something more from her staid life.

About the Author

Lily Harlem

Lily Harlem lives in the UK with a workaholic hunk and a crazy cat. With a desk overlooking rolling hills her over active imagination has been allowed to run wild and free and she revels in using the written word as an outlet for her creativity.

Natalie Dae

Natalie Dae is a multi-published author in three pen names writing in several genres. Natalie writes mainly BDSM erotica. She loves a Dom/sub relationship and is fascinated by how it all works. The trust issue is the best thing about it for her, so creating characters who have to adopt trust is one of her priorities. "Watching my characters bloom under tuition is such a treat," she says. "I find it such a privilege to be able to write about something that makes me learn something new with every book."

She lives with her husband and youngest daughter in England and spends her spare time reading—always reading!—and her phone, complete with Kindle app, is never far away. "I can't imagine not reading or writing," she says. "It's a part of who I am. Without it I'd be more than a bit lost."

Natalie has many more BDSM tales swimming around in her head, so her workload for the future is very full. "What better way to spend a weekend than writing?" she says. "Saturdays are my main writing days, so I get up, open up a work in progress and rarely leave the desk. Unless I really have to!"

She writes at weekends and is a cover artist/head of art in her day job. In another life she was an editor. Her other pen names are Geraldine O'Hara and Sarah Masters. Natalie also co-authors as Sarah Masters with Jaime Samms, and she co-authors with Lily Harlem under the name Harlem Dae.

Lily's stories are made up of colourful characters exploring their sexuality and sensuality in a safe, consensual way. With the bedroom door left wide open the reader can hang on for the ride and Lily hopes by reading sensual romance people will be brave enough to try something new themselves? After all, life's too short to be anything other than fully satisfied.

Our authors love to hear from readers. You can find contact information, website details and an author profile page at https://www.totallybound.com/

TOTALLY
BOUND
Home of Erotic Romance